The Frozen Deep

The Frozen Deep

Wilkie Collins

Hesperus Classics

Hesperus Classics
Published by Hesperus Press Limited
4 Rickett Street, London SW6 1RU
www.hesperuspress.com

First published in *Temple Bar* in 1874
First published by Hesperus Press Limited, 2004
Reprinted 2005

Designed and typeset by Fraser Muggeridge
Printed in Jordan by Jordan National Press

ISBN: 1-84391-0-94-2

CONTENTS

The Frozen Deep

CHAPTER ONE

The date is between twenty and thirty years ago. The place is an English seaport. The time is night. And the business of the moment is – dancing.

The mayor and corporation of the town are giving a grand ball, in celebration of the departure of an Arctic expedition from their port. The ships of the expedition are two in number – the *Wanderer* and the *Sea-mew*. They are to sail (in search of the North-West Passage) on the next day, with the morning tide.

Honour to the mayor and corporation! It is a brilliant ball. The band is complete. The room is spacious. The large conservatory opening out of it is pleasantly lit with Chinese lanterns, and beautifully decorated with shrubs and flowers. All officers of the army and navy who are present wear their uniforms in honour of the occasion. Among the ladies, the display of dresses (a subject which the men don't understand) is bewildering – and the average of beauty (a subject which the men do understand) is the highest average attainable, in all parts of the room.

For the moment, the dance which is in progress is a quadrille. General admiration selects two of the ladies who are dancing as its favourite objects. One is a dark beauty in the prime of womanhood – the wife of First Lieutenant Crayford of the *Wanderer*. The other is a young girl, pale and delicate; dressed simply in white; with no ornament on her head but her own lovely brown hair. This is Miss Clara Burnham – an orphan. She is Mrs Crayford's dearest friend, and she is to stay with Mrs Crayford during the lieutenant's absence in the Arctic regions. She is now dancing, with the lieutenant himself for partner, and with Mrs Crayford and Captain Helding (commanding officer of the *Wanderer*) for vis-à-vis – in plain English, for opposite couple.

The conversation between Captain Helding and Mrs Crayford, in one of the intervals of the dance, turns on Miss Burnham. The captain is greatly interested in Clara. He admires her beauty, but he thinks her manner – for a young girl – strangely serious and subdued. Is she in delicate health?

Mrs Crayford shakes her head; sighs mysteriously; and answers, 'In *very* delicate health, Captain Helding.'

'Consumptive?'

'Not in the least.'

'I am glad to hear that. She is a charming creature, Mrs Crayford. She interests me indescribably. If I was only twenty years younger – perhaps (as I am not twenty years younger) I had better not finish the sentence? Is it indiscreet, my dear lady, to enquire what *is* the matter with her?'

'It might be indiscreet, on the part of a stranger,' said Mrs Crayford. 'An old friend like you may make any enquiries. I wish I could tell you what is the matter with Clara. It is a mystery to the doctors themselves. Some of the mischief is due, in my humble opinion, to the manner in which she has been brought up.'

'Ay! ay! A bad school, I suppose.'

'Very bad, Captain Helding. But not the sort of school which you have in your mind at this moment. Clara's early years were spent in a lonely old house in the Highlands of Scotland. The ignorant people about her were the people who did the mischief which I have just been speaking of. They filled her mind with the superstitions which are still respected as truths in the wild North – especially the superstition called the Second Sight.'

'God bless me!' cried the captain, 'you don't mean to say she believes in such stuff as that? In these enlightened times too!'

Mrs Crayford looked at her partner with a satirical smile.

'In these enlightened times, Captain Helding, we only believe in dancing tables, and in messages sent from the other world by spirits who can't spell! By comparison with such superstitions as these, even the Second Sight has something – in the shape of poetry – to recommend it, surely? Estimate for yourself,' she continued seriously, 'the effect of such surroundings as I have described on a delicate, sensitive young creature – a girl with a naturally imaginative temperament leading a lonely, neglected life. Is it so very surprising that she should catch the infection of the superstition about her? And is it quite incomprehensible that her nervous system should suffer accordingly, at a very critical period of her life?'

'Not at all, Mrs Crayford – not at all, ma'am, as you put it. Still it is a little startling, to a commonplace man like me, to meet a young lady at a ball who believes in the Second Sight. Does she really profess to see into the future? Am I to understand that she positively falls into a trance, and sees people in distant countries, and foretells events to come? That is the Second Sight, is it not?'

'That is the Second Sight, Captain. And that is, really and positively, what she does.'

'The young lady who is dancing opposite to us?'

'The young lady who is dancing opposite to us.'

The captain waited a little – letting the new flood of information which had poured in on him settle itself steadily in his mind. This process accomplished, the Arctic explorer proceeded resolutely on his way to further discoveries.

'May I ask, ma'am, if you have ever seen her in a state of trance with your own eyes?' he enquired.

'My sister and I both saw her in the trance, little more than a month since,' Mrs Crayford replied. 'She had been nervous and irritable all the morning; and we took her out into the garden to breathe the fresh air. Suddenly, without any reason for it, the colour left her face. She stood between us, insensible to touch, insensible to sound, motionless as stone, and cold as death in a moment. The first change we noticed came after a lapse of some minutes. Her hands began to move slowly, as if she was groping in the dark. Words dropped one by one from her lips, in a lost, vacant tone, as if she was talking in her sleep. Whether what she said referred to past or future I cannot tell you. She spoke of persons in a foreign country – perfect strangers to my sister and to me. After a little interval, she suddenly became silent. A momentary colour appeared in her face, and left it again. Her eyes closed – her feet failed her – and she sank insensible into our arms.'

'Sank insensible into your arms,' repeated the captain, absorbing his new information. 'Most extraordinary! And – in this state of health – she goes out to parties, and dances. More extraordinary still!'

'You are entirely mistaken,' said Mrs Crayford. 'She is only here tonight to please me; and she is only dancing to please my husband. As a rule, she shuns all society. The doctor recommends change and amusement for her. She won't listen to him. Except on rare occasions like this, she persists in remaining at home.'

Captain Helding brightened at the allusion to the doctor. Something practical might be got out of the doctor. Scientific man. Sure to see this very obscure subject under a new light. 'How does it strike the doctor now?' said the captain. 'Viewed simply as a case, ma'am, how does it strike the doctor?'

'He will give no positive opinion,' Mrs Crayford answered. 'He told me that such cases as Clara's were by no means unfamiliar to medical practice. "We know," he told me, "that certain disordered conditions of the brain and the nervous system produce results quite as extraordinary as any that you have described – and there our knowledge ends. Neither my science nor any man's science can clear up the mystery in this case. It is an especially difficult case to deal with, because Miss Burnham's early associations dispose her to attach a superstitious importance to the malady – the hysterical malady as some doctors would call it – from which she suffers. I can give you instructions for preserving her general health; and I can recommend you to try some change in her life – provided you first relieve her mind of any secret anxieties that may possibly be preying on it."'

The captain smiled self-approvingly. The doctor had justified his anticipations. The doctor had suggested a practical solution to the difficulty.

'Ay! ay! At last we have hit the nail on the head! Secret anxieties. Yes! yes! Plain enough now. A disappointment in love – eh, Mrs Crayford?'

'I don't know, Captain Helding; I am quite in the dark. Clara's confidence in me – in other matters unbounded – is, in this matter of her (supposed) anxieties, a confidence still withheld. In all else we are like sisters. I sometimes fear there may indeed be some trouble preying secretly on her mind. I sometimes feel a little hurt at her incomprehensible silence.'

Captain Helding was ready with his own practical remedy for this difficulty.

'Encouragement is all she wants, ma'am. Take my word for it, this matter rests entirely with you. It's all in a nutshell. Encourage her to confide in you – and she *will* confide.'

'I am waiting to encourage her, Captain, until she is left alone with me – after you have all sailed for the Arctic seas. In the meantime, will you consider what I have said to you as intended for your ear only? And will you forgive me if I own that the turn the subject has taken does not tempt me to pursue it any further?'

The captain took the hint. He instantly changed the subject; choosing, on this occasion, safe professional topics. He spoke of ships that were ordered on foreign service; and, finding that these as subjects failed to interest Mrs Crayford, he spoke next of ships that were ordered home again. This last experiment produced its effect – an effect which the captain had not bargained for.

'Do you know,' he began, 'that the *Atalanta* is expected back from the West Coast of Africa every day? Have you any acquaintances among the officers of that ship?'

As it so happened, he put those questions to Mrs Crayford while they were engaged in one of the figures of the dance which brought them within hearing of the opposite couple. At the same moment – to the astonishment of her friends and admirers – Miss Clara Burnham threw the quadrille into confusion by making a mistake! Everybody waited to see her set the mistake right. She made no attempt to set it right – she turned deadly pale and caught her partner by the arm.

'The heat!' she said, faintly. 'Take me away – take me into the air!'

Lieutenant Crayford instantly led her out of the dance, and took her into the cool and empty conservatory at the end of the room. As a matter of course, Captain Helding and Mrs Crayford left the quadrille at the same time. The captain saw his way to a joke.

'Is this the trance coming on?' he whispered. 'If it is, as commander of the Arctic expedition, I have a particular request to make. Will the Second Sight oblige me by seeing the shortest way to the North-West Passage, before we leave England?'

Mrs Crayford declined to humour the joke. 'If you will excuse my leaving you,' she said quietly, 'I will try and find out what is the matter with Miss Burnham.'

At the entrance to the conservatory, Mrs Crayford encountered her husband. The lieutenant was of middle age, tall and comely. A man with a winning simplicity and gentleness in his manner, and an irresistible kindness in his brave blue eyes. In one word, a man whom everybody loved – including his wife.

'Don't be alarmed,' said the lieutenant. 'The heat has overcome her – that's all.'

Mrs Crayford shook her head, and looked at her husband, half satirically, half fondly.

'You dear old innocent!' she exclaimed, 'that excuse may do for *you*. For my part, I don't believe a word of it. Go and get another partner, and leave Clara to me.'

She entered the conservatory and seated herself by Clara's side.

CHAPTER TWO

'Now, my dear!' Mrs Crayford began, 'what does this mean?'

'Nothing.'

'That won't do, Clara. Try again.'

'The heat of the room –'

'That won't do, either. Say that you choose to keep your own secrets, and I shall understand what you mean.'

Clara's sad, clear grey eyes looked up for the first time into Mrs Crayford's face, and suddenly became dimmed with tears.

'If I only dared tell you!' she murmured. 'I hold so to your good opinion of me, Lucy – and I am so afraid of losing it.'

Mrs Crayford's manner changed. Her eyes rested gravely and anxiously on Clara's face.

'You know as well as I do that nothing can shake my affection for you,' she said. 'Do justice, my child, to your old friend. There is nobody here to listen to what we say. Open your heart, Clara. I see you are in trouble, and I want to comfort you.'

Clara began to yield. In other words, she began to make conditions.

'Will you promise to keep what I tell you a secret from every living creature?' she began.

Mrs Crayford met that question by putting a question on her side.

'Does "every living creature" include my husband?'

'Your husband more than anybody! I love him, I revere him. He is so noble – he is so good! If I told him what I am going to tell you, he would despise me. Own it plainly, Lucy, if I am asking too much in asking you to keep a secret from your husband.'

'Nonsense, child! When you are married, you will know

that the easiest of all secrets to keep is a secret from your husband. I give you my promise. Now begin!'

Clara hesitated painfully.

'I don't know how to begin!' she exclaimed, with a burst of despair. 'The words won't come to me.'

'Then I must help you. Do you feel ill tonight? Do you feel as you felt that day when you were with my sister and me in the garden?'

'Oh no.'

'You are not ill, you are not really affected by the heat – and yet you turn as pale as ashes, and you are obliged to leave the quadrille! There must be some reason for this.'

'There is a reason. Captain Helding –'

'Captain Helding! What in the name of wonder has the captain to do with it?'

'He told you something about the *Atalanta*. He said the *Atalanta* was expected back from Africa immediately.'

'Well, and what of that? Is there anybody in whom you are interested coming home in the ship?'

'Somebody whom I am afraid of is coming home in the ship.'

Mrs Crayford's magnificent black eyes opened wide in amazement.

'My dear Clara! do you really mean what you say?'

'Wait a little, Lucy, and you shall judge for yourself. We must go back – if I am to make you understand me – to the year before we knew each other – to the last year of my father's life. Did I ever tell you that my father moved southward, for the sake of his health, to a house in Kent that was lent to him by a friend?'

'No, my dear; I don't remember ever hearing of the house in Kent. Tell me about it.'

'There is nothing to tell, except this: the new house was near a fine country seat standing in its own park. The owner of the place was a gentleman named Wardour. He, too, was one of my father's Kentish friends. He had an only son.'

She paused, and played nervously with her fan. Mrs Crayford looked at her attentively. Clara's eyes remained fixed on her fan – Clara said no more.

'What was the son's name?' asked Mrs Crayford, quietly.

'Richard.'

'Am I right, Clara, in suspecting that Mr Richard Wardour admired you?'

The question produced its intended effect. The question helped Clara to go on.

'I hardly knew at first,' she said, 'whether he admired me or not. He was very strange in his ways – headstrong, terribly headstrong and passionate; but generous and affectionate in spite of his faults of temper. Can you understand such a character?'

'Such characters exist by thousands. I have my faults of temper. I begin to like Richard already. Go on.'

'The days went by, Lucy, and the weeks went by. We were thrown very much together. I began, little by little, to have some suspicion of the truth.'

'And Richard helped to confirm your suspicions, of course?'

'No. He was not – unhappily for me – he was not that sort of man. He never spoke of the feeling with which he regarded me. It was I who saw it. I couldn't help seeing it. I did all I could to show that I was willing to be a sister to him, and that I could never be anything else. He did not understand me, or he would not, I can't say which.'

' "Would not" is the most likely, my dear. Go on.'

'It might have been as you say. There was a strange, rough bashfulness about him. He confused and puzzled me. He never spoke out. He seemed to treat me as if our future lives had been provided for while we were children. What could I do, Lucy?'

'Do? You could have asked your father to end the difficulty for you.'

'Impossible! You forget what I have just told you. My father was suffering at that time under the illness which afterwards caused his death. He was quite unfit to interfere.'

'Was there no one else who could help you?'

'No one.'

'No lady in whom you could confide?'

'I had acquaintances among the ladies in the neighbourhood. I had no friends.'

'What did you do, then?'

'Nothing. I hesitated; I put off coming to an explanation with him, unfortunately, until it was too late.'

'What do you mean by too late?'

'You shall hear. I ought to have told you that Richard Wardour is in the navy.'

'Indeed! I am more interested in him than ever. Well?'

'One spring day Richard came to our house to take leave of us before he joined his ship. I thought he was gone, and I went into the next room. It was my own sitting room, and it opened onto the garden.'

'Yes?'

'Richard must have been watching me. He suddenly appeared in the garden. Without waiting for me to invite him, he walked into the room. I was a little startled as well as surprised, but I managed to hide it. I said, "What is it, Mr Wardour?" He stepped close up to me; he said, in his quick, rough way: "Clara! I am going to the African coast. If I live, I shall come back promoted; and we both know what will happen then." He kissed me. I was half frightened, half angry. Before I could compose myself to say a word, he was out in the garden again – he was gone! I ought to have spoken, I know. It was not honourable, not kind towards him. You can't reproach me for my want of courage and frankness more bitterly than I reproach myself!'

'My dear child, I don't reproach you. I only think you might have written to him.'

'I did write.'

'Plainly?'

'Yes. I told him in so many words that he was deceiving himself, and that I could never marry him.'

'Plain enough, in all conscience! Having said that, surely you are not to blame. What are you fretting about now?'

'Suppose my letter has never reached him?'

'Why should you suppose anything of the sort?'

'What I wrote required an answer, Lucy – *asked* for an answer. The answer has never come. What is the plain conclusion? My letter has never reached him. And the *Atalanta* is expected back! Richard Wardour is returning to England – Richard Wardour will claim me as his wife! You wondered just now if I really meant what I said. Do you doubt it still?'

Mrs Crayford leant back absently in her chair. For the first time since the conversation had begun, she let a question pass without making a reply. The truth is, Mrs Crayford was thinking.

She saw Clara's position plainly; she understood the disturbing effect of it on the mind of a young girl. Still, making all allowances, she felt quite at a loss, so far, to account for Clara's excessive agitation. Her quick observing faculty had just detected that Clara's face showed no signs of relief, now that she had unburdened herself of her secret. There was something clearly under the surface here – something of importance that still remained to be discovered. A shrewd doubt crossed Mrs Crayford's mind, and inspired the next words which she addressed to her young friend.

'My dear,' she said abruptly, 'have you told me all?'

Clara started as if the question terrified her. Feeling sure that she now had the clue in her hand, Mrs Crayford deliberately repeated her question, in another form of words. Instead of answering, Clara suddenly looked up. At the same moment a faint flush of colour appeared in her face for the first time.

Looking up instinctively on her side, Mrs Crayford became aware of the presence, in the conservatory, of a young gentleman who was claiming Clara as his partner in the coming waltz. Mrs Crayford fell into thinking once more. Had this young gentleman (she asked herself) anything to do with the untold end of the story? Was this the true secret of Clara Burnham's terror at the impending return of Richard Wardour? Mrs Crayford decided on putting her doubts to the test.

'A friend of yours, my dear?' she asked, innocently. 'Suppose you introduce us to each other?'

Clara confusedly introduced the young gentleman.

'Mr Francis Aldersley, Lucy. Mr Aldersley belongs to the Arctic expedition.'

'Attached to the expedition?' Mrs Crayford repeated. 'I am attached to the expedition too – in my way. I had better introduce myself, Mr Aldersley, as Clara seems to have forgotten to do it for me. I am Mrs Crayford. My husband is Lieutenant Crayford of the *Wanderer*. Do you belong to that ship?'

'I have not the honour, Mrs Crayford. I belong to the *Sea-mew*.'

Mrs Crayford's superb eyes looked shrewdly backwards and forwards between Clara and Francis Aldersley, and saw the untold sequel to Clara's story. The young officer was a bright, handsome, gentleman-like lad. Just the person to seriously complicate the difficulty with Richard Wardour! There was no time for making any further enquiries. The band had begun the prelude to the waltz, and Francis Aldersley was waiting for his partner. With a word of apology to the young man, Mrs Crayford drew Clara aside for a moment, and spoke to her in a whisper.

'One word, my dear, before you return to the ballroom. It may sound conceited, after the little you have told me; but I think I understand your position *now* better than you do yourself. Do you want to hear my opinion?'

'I am longing to hear it, Lucy! I want your opinion; I want your advice.'

'You shall have both in the plainest and fewest words. First, my opinion: you have no choice but to come to an explanation with Mr Wardour as soon as he returns. Second, my advice: if you wish to make the explanation easy to both sides, take care that you make it in the character of a free woman.'

She laid a strong emphasis on the last three words, and looked pointedly at Francis Aldersley as she pronounced them. 'I won't keep you from your partner any longer, Clara,' she resumed, and led the way back to the ballroom.

CHAPTER THREE

The burden on Clara's mind weighs on it more heavily than ever, after what Mrs Crayford has said to her. She is too unhappy to feel the inspiriting influence of the dance. After a turn round the room, she complains of fatigue. Mr Francis Aldersley looks at the conservatory (still as invitingly cool and empty as ever); leads her back to it; and places her on a seat among the shrubs.

She tries – very feebly – to dismiss him.

'Don't let me keep you from dancing, Mr Aldersley.'

He seats himself by her side, and feasts his eyes on the lovely downcast face that dares not turn towards him. He whispers to her:

'Call me Frank.'

She longs to call him Frank – she loves him with all her heart. But Mrs Crayford's warning words are still in her mind. She never opens her lips. Her lover moves a little closer, and asks another favour. Men are all alike on these occasions. Silence invariably encourages them to try again.

'Clara! have you forgotten what I said at the concert yesterday? May I say it again?'

'No!'

'We sail tomorrow for the Arctic seas. I may not return for years. Don't send me away without hope! Think of the long, lonely time in the dark North! Make it a happy time for *me*.'

Though he speaks with the fervour of a man, he is little more than a lad: he is only twenty years old, and he is going to risk his young life on the Frozen Deep! Clara pities him as she never pitied any human creature before. He gently takes her hand. She tries to release it.

'What! not even that little favour on the last night?'

Her faithful heart takes his part, in spite of her. Her hand remains in his, and feels its soft persuasive pressure. She is a lost woman. It is only a question of time now!

'Clara! do you love me?'

There is a pause. She shrinks from looking at him – she trembles with strange contradictory sensations of pleasure and pain. His arm steals round her; he repeats his question in a whisper; his lips almost touch her little rosy ear as he says it again:

'Do you love me?'

She closes her eyes faintly – she hears nothing but those words – feels nothing but his arm round her – forgets Mrs Crayford's warning – forgets Richard Wardour himself – turns suddenly, with a loving woman's desperate disregard of everything but her love – nestles her head on his bosom, and answers him in that way, at last!

He lifts the beautiful drooping head – their lips meet in their first kiss – they are both in heaven: it is Clara who brings them back to earth again with a start – it is Clara who says, 'Oh! what have I done?' – as usual, when it is too late.

Frank answers the question.

'You have made me happy, my angel. Now, when I come back, I come back to make you my wife.'

She shudders. She remembers Richard Wardour again at those words.

'Mind!' she says, 'nobody is to know we are engaged till I permit you to mention it. Remember that!'

He promises to remember it. His arm tries to wind round her once more. No! She is mistress of herself; she can positively dismiss him now – after she has let him kiss her!

'Go!' she says. 'I want to see Mrs Crayford. Find her! Say

I am here, waiting to speak to her. Go at once, Frank – for my sake!'

There is no alternative but to obey her. His eyes drink a last draught of her beauty. He hurries away on his errand – the happiest man in the room. Five minutes since she was only his partner in the dance. He has spoken – and she has pledged herself to be his partner for life!

CHAPTER FOUR

It was not easy to find Mrs Crayford in the crowd. Searching here, and searching there, Frank became conscious of a stranger, who appeared to be looking for somebody, at his side. He was a dark, heavy-browed, strongly built man, dressed in a shabby old naval officer's uniform. His manner – strikingly resolute and self-contained – was unmistakably the manner of a gentleman. He wound his way slowly through the crowd; stopping to look at every lady whom he passed, and then looking away again with a frown. Little by little he approached the conservatory – entered it, after a moment's reflection – detected the glimmer of a white dress in the distance, through the shrubs and flowers – advanced to get a nearer view of the lady – and burst into Clara's presence with a cry of delight.

She sprang to her feet. She stood before him speechless, motionless, struck to stone. All her life was in her eyes – the eyes which told her she was looking at Richard Wardour.

He was the first to speak.

'I am sorry I startled you, my darling. I forgot everything but the happiness of seeing you again. We only reached our moorings two hours since. I was some time enquiring after you, and some time getting my ticket when they told me you were at the ball. Wish me joy, Clara! I am promoted. I have come back to make you my wife.'

A momentary change passed over the blank terror of her face. Her colour rose faintly, her lips moved. She abruptly put a question to him.

'Did you get my letter?'

He started. 'A letter from you? I never received it.'

The momentary animation died out of her face again. She

drew back from him and dropped into a chair. He advanced towards her, astonished and alarmed. She shrank in the chair – shrank, as if she was frightened of him.

'Clara, you have not even shaken hands with me! What does it mean?'

He paused; waiting and watching her. She made no reply. A flash of the quick temper in him leapt up in his eyes. He repeated his last words in louder and sterner tones:

'What does it mean?'

She replied this time. His tone had hurt her – his tone had roused her sinking courage.

'It means, Mr Wardour, that you have been mistaken from the first.'

'How have I been mistaken?'

'You have been under a wrong impression, and you have given me no opportunity of setting you right.'

'In what way have I been wrong?'

'You have been too hasty and too confident about yourself and about me. You have entirely misunderstood me. I am grieved to distress you, but for your sake I must speak plainly. I am your friend always, Mr Wardour. I can never be your wife.'

He mechanically repeated the last words. He seemed to doubt whether he had heard her aright.

'You can never be my wife?'

'Never!'

'Why?'

There was no answer. She was incapable of telling him a falsehood. She was ashamed to tell him the truth.

He stooped over her, and suddenly possessed himself of her hand. Holding her hand firmly, he stooped a little lower; searching for the signs which might answer him in her face. His own face darkened slowly while he looked. He was beginning to suspect her; and he acknowledged it in his next words.

'Something has changed you towards me, Clara. Somebody has influenced you against me. Is it – you force me to ask the question – is it some other man?'

'You have no right to ask me that.'

He went on without noticing what she had said to him.

'Has that other man come between you and me? I speak plainly on my side. Speak plainly on yours.'

'I *have* spoken. I have nothing more to say.'

There was a pause. She saw the warning light which told of the fire within him growing brighter and brighter in his eyes. She felt his grasp strengthening on her hand. He appealed to her for the last time.

'Reflect,' he said, 'reflect before it is too late. Your silence will not serve you. If you persist in not answering me, I shall take your silence as a confession. Do you hear me?'

'I hear you.'

'Clara Burnham! I am not to be trifled with. Clara Burnham! I insist on the truth. Are you false to me?'

She resented that searching question with a woman's keen sense of the insult that is implied in doubting her to her face.

'Mr Wardour! you forget yourself when you call me to account in that way. I never encouraged you. I never gave you promise or pledge –'

He passionately interrupted her before she could say more.

'You have engaged yourself in my absence. Your words own it; your looks own it! You have engaged yourself to another man!'

'If I *have* engaged myself, what right have you to complain of it?' she answered firmly. 'What right have you to control my actions?…'

The next words died away on her lips. He suddenly dropped her hand. A marked change appeared in the expression of his eyes – a change which told her of the terrible passions that she had let loose in him. She read, dimly read, something in his face which made her tremble – not for herself, but for Frank.

Little by little the dark colour faded out of his face. His deep voice dropped suddenly to a low and quiet tone as he spoke the parting words.

'Say no more, Miss Burnham – you have said enough. I am answered; I am dismissed.' He paused and, stepping close up to her, laid his hand on her arm.

'The time may come,' he said, 'when I shall forgive you. But the man who has robbed me of you shall rue the day when you and he first met.'

He turned and left her.

A few minutes later, Mrs Crayford, entering the conservatory, was met by one of the attendants at the ball. The man stopped as if he wished to speak to her.

'What do you want?' she asked.

'I beg your pardon, ma'am. Do you happen to have a smelling bottle about you? There is a young lady in the conservatory who is taken faint.'

CHAPTER FIVE

The morning of the next day – the morning on which the ships were to sail – came bright and breezy. Mrs Crayford, having arranged to follow her husband to the waterside, and see the last of him before he embarked, entered Clara's room on her way out of the house, anxious to hear how her young friend passed the night. To her astonishment she found Clara had risen, and was dressed, like herself, to go out.

'What does this mean, my dear? After what you suffered last night – after the shock of seeing that man – why don't you take my advice and rest in your bed?'

'I can't rest. I have not slept all night. Have you been out yet?'

'No.'

'Have you seen or heard anything of Richard Wardour?'

'What an extraordinary question!'

'Answer my question! Don't trifle with me!'

'Compose yourself, Clara. I have neither seen nor heard anything of Richard Wardour. Take my word for it, he is far enough away by this time.'

'No! He is here! He is near us! All night long the presentiment has pursued me – Frank and Richard Wardour will meet.'

'My dear child! what are you thinking of? They are total strangers to each other.'

'Something will happen to bring them together. I feel it! I know it! They will meet – there will be a mortal quarrel between them – and I shall be to blame. Oh, Lucy! why didn't I take your advice? Why was I mad enough to let Frank know that I loved him? Are you going to the landing stage? I am all ready – I must go with you.'

'You must not think of it, Clara. There will be crowding and confusion at the waterside. You are not strong enough to bear it. Wait – I won't be long away – wait till I come back.'

'I must and will go with you! Crowd? *He* will be among the crowd! Confusion? In that confusion *he* will find his way to Frank! Don't ask me to wait. I shall go mad if I wait. I shall not know a moment's ease until I have seen Frank, with my own eyes, safe in the boat which takes him to his ship! You have got your bonnet on; what are we stopping here for? Come! or I shall go without you. Look at the clock; we have not a moment to lose!'

It was useless to contend with her. Mrs Crayford yielded. The two women left the house together.

The landing stage, as Mrs Crayford had predicted, was thronged with spectators. Not only the relatives and friends of the Arctic voyagers, but strangers as well, had assembled in large numbers to see the ships sail. Clara's eyes wandered affrightedly hither and thither among the strange faces in the crowd; searching for the one face that she dreaded to see, and not finding it. So completely were her nerves unstrung that she started with a cry of alarm on suddenly hearing Frank's voice behind her.

'The *Sea-mew*'s boats are waiting,' he said. 'I must go, darling. How pale you are looking, Clara! Are you ill?'

She never answered. She questioned him with wild eyes and trembling lips.

'Has anything happened to you, Frank? Anything out of the common?'

Frank laughed at the strange question.

'Anything out of the common?' he repeated. 'Nothing that I know of, except sailing for the Arctic seas. That's out of the common, I suppose – isn't it?'

'Has anybody spoken to you since last night? Has any

stranger followed you in the street?'

Frank turned in blank amazement to Mrs Crayford.

'What on earth does she mean?'

Mrs Crayford's lively invention supplied her with an answer on the spur of the moment.

'Do you believe in dreams, Frank? Of course you don't! Clara has been dreaming about you; and Clara is foolish enough to believe in dreams. That's all – it's not worth talking about. Hark! they are calling you. Say goodbye, or you will be too late for the boat.'

Frank took Clara's hand. Long afterwards – in the dark Arctic days, in the dreary Arctic nights – he remembered how coldly and how passively that hand lay in his.

'Courage, Clara!' he said, gaily. 'A sailor's sweetheart must accustom herself to partings. The time will soon pass. Goodbye, my darling! Goodbye, my wife!'

He kissed the cold hand; he looked his last – for many a long year, perhaps! – at the pale and beautiful face. 'How she loves me!' he thought. 'How the parting distresses her!' He still held her hand; he would have lingered longer if Mrs Crayford had not wisely waived all ceremony and pushed him away.

The two ladies followed him at a safe distance through the crowd, and saw him step into the boat. The oars struck the water; Frank waved his cap to Clara. In a moment more a vessel at anchor hid the boat from view. They had seen the last of him on his way to the Frozen Deep!

'No Richard Wardour in the boat,' said Mrs Crayford. 'No Richard Wardour on the shore. Let this be a lesson to you, my dear. Never be foolish enough to believe in presentiments again.'

Clara's eyes still wandered suspiciously to and fro among the crowd.

'Are you not satisfied yet?' asked Mrs Crayford.

'No,' Clara answered, 'I am not satisfied yet.'

'What! still looking for him? This is really too absurd. Here is my husband coming. I shall tell him to call a cab, and send you home.'

Clara drew back a few steps.

'I won't be in the way, Lucy, while you are taking leave of your good husband,' she said. 'I will wait here.'

'Wait here! What for?'

'For something which I may yet see; or for something which I may still hear.'

'Richard Wardour?'

'Richard Wardour.'

Mrs Crayford turned to her husband without another word. Clara's infatuation was beyond the reach of remonstrance.

The boats of the *Wanderer* took the place at the landing stage vacated by the boats of the *Sea-mew*. A burst of cheering among the outer ranks of the crowd announced the arrival of the commander of the expedition on the scene. Captain Helding appeared, looking right and left for his first lieutenant.

Finding Crayford with his wife, the captain made his apologies for interfering, with his best grace.

'Give him up to his professional duties for one minute, Mrs Crayford, and you shall have him back again for half an hour. The Arctic expedition is to blame, my dear lady – not the captain – for parting man and wife. In Crayford's place, I should have left it to the bachelors to find the North-West Passage, and have stopped at home with you!'

Excusing himself in those bluntly complimentary terms, Captain Helding drew the lieutenant aside a few steps, accidentally taking a direction that led the two officers close to the place at which Clara was standing. Both the captain and the lieutenant were too completely absorbed in their professional business to notice her. Neither the one nor the other had the faintest suspicion that she could and did hear every word of the talk that passed between them.

'You received my note this morning?' the captain began.

'Certainly, Captain Helding, or I should have been on board the ship before this.'

'I am going on board myself at once,' the captain proceeded, 'but I must ask you to keep your boat waiting for half an hour more. You will be all the longer with your wife, you know. I thought of that, Crayford.'

'I am much obliged to you, Captain Helding. I suppose there is some other reason for inverting the customary order of things, and keeping the lieutenant on shore after the captain is on board?'

'Quite true! there *is* another reason. I want you to wait for a volunteer who has just joined us.'

'A volunteer!'

'Yes. He has his outfit to get in a hurry, and he may be half an hour late.'

'It's rather a sudden appointment, isn't it?'

'No doubt. Very sudden.'

'And – pardon me – it's rather a long time (as we are situated) to keep the ships waiting for one man?'

'Quite true, again. But a man who is worth having is worth waiting for. This man is worth having; this man is worth his weight in gold to such an expedition as ours. Seasoned to all climates and all fatigues – a strong fellow, a brave fellow, a clever fellow – in short, an excellent officer. I know him well, or I should never have taken him. The country gets plenty of work out of my new volunteer, Crayford. He only returned yesterday from foreign service.'

'He only returned yesterday from foreign service! And he volunteers this morning to join the Arctic expedition? You astonish me.'

'I dare say I do! You can't be more astonished than I was when he presented himself at my hotel and told me what he wanted. "Why, my good fellow, you have just got home," I said. "Are you weary of your freedom, after only a few hours' experience of it?" His answer rather startled me. He said, "I am weary of my life, sir. I have come home and found a trouble to welcome me which goes near to break my heart. If I don't take refuge in absence and hard work, I am a lost man. Will you give me a refuge?" That's what he said, Crayford, word for word.'

'Did you ask him to explain himself further?'

'Not I! I knew his value, and I took the poor devil on the spot, without pestering him with any more questions. No need to ask him to explain himself. The facts speak for themselves in these cases. The old story, my good friend! There's a woman at the bottom of it, of course.'

Mrs Crayford, waiting for the return of her husband as patiently as she could, was startled by feeling a hand suddenly laid on her shoulder. She looked round, and confronted Clara. Her first feeling of surprise changed instantly to alarm. Clara was trembling from head to foot.

'What is the matter? What has frightened you, my dear?'

'Lucy! I *have* heard of him!'

'Richard Wardour again?'

'Remember what I told you. I have heard every word of the conversation between Captain Helding and your husband. A man came to the captain this morning and volunteered to join the *Wanderer*. The captain has taken him.

The man is Richard Wardour.'

'You don't mean it! Are you sure? Did you hear Captain Helding mention his name?'

'No.'

'Then how do you know it's Richard Wardour?'

'Don't ask me! I am as certain of it as that I am standing here! They are going away together, Lucy – away to the eternal ice and snow. My foreboding has come true! The two will meet – the man who is to marry me and the man whose heart I have broken!'

'Your foreboding has *not* come true, Clara! The men have not met here – the men are not likely to meet elsewhere. They are appointed to separate ships. Frank belongs to the *Sea-mew*, and Wardour to the *Wanderer*. See! Captain Helding has done. My husband is coming this way. Let me make sure. Let me speak to him.'

Lieutenant Crayford returned to his wife. She spoke to him instantly.

'William! you have got a new volunteer who joins the *Wanderer*?'

'What! you have been listening to the captain and me?'

'I want to know his name?'

'How in the world did you manage to hear what we said to each other?'

'His name? Has the captain given you his name?'

'Don't excite yourself, my dear. Look! you are positively alarming Miss Burnham. The new volunteer is a perfect stranger to us. There is his name – last on the ship's list.'

Mrs Crayford snatched the list out of her husband's hand and read the name:

'Richard Wardour.'

CHAPTER SIX

Goodbye to England! Goodbye to inhabited and civilised regions of the earth!

Two years have passed since the voyagers sailed from their native shores. The enterprise has failed – the Arctic expedition is lost and ice-locked in the Polar wastes. The good ships *Wanderer* and *Sea-mew*, entombed in ice, will never ride the buoyant waters more. Stripped of their lighter timbers, both vessels have been used for the construction of huts, erected on the nearest land.

The largest of the two buildings which now shelter the lost men is occupied by the surviving officers and crew of the *Sea-mew*. On one side of the principal room are the sleeping berths and the fireplace. The other side discloses a broad doorway (closed by a canvas screen) which serves as a means of communication with an inner apartment, devoted to the superior officers. A hammock is slung to the rough raftered roof of the main room as an extra bed. A man, completely hidden by his bedclothes, is sleeping in the hammock. By the fireside there is a second man – supposed to be on the watch – fast asleep, poor wretch!, at the present moment. Behind the sleeper stands an old cask which serves for a table. The objects at present on the table are a pestle and mortar, and a saucepanful of the dry bones of animals – in plain words, the dinner for the day. By way of ornament to the dull brown walls, icicles appear in the crevices of the timber, gleaming at intervals in the red firelight. No wind whistles outside the lonely dwelling – no cry of bird or beast is heard. Indoors, and out of doors, the awful silence of the Polar desert reigns, for the moment, undisturbed.

CHAPTER SEVEN

The first sound that broke the silence came from the inner apartment. An officer lifted the canvas screen in the hut of the *Sea-mew* and entered the main room. Cold and privation had badly thinned the ranks. The commander of the ship – Captain Ebsworth – was dangerously ill. The first lieutenant was dead. An officer of the *Wanderer* filled their places for the time, with Captain Helding's permission. The officer so employed was – Lieutenant Crayford.

He approached the man at the fireside, and awakened him.

'Jump up, Bateson! It's your turn to be relieved.'

The relief appeared, rising from a heap of old sails at the back of the hut. Bateson vanished, yawning, to his bed. Lieutenant Crayford walked backwards and forwards briskly, trying what exercise would do towards warming his blood.

The pestle and mortar on the cask attracted his attention. He stopped and looked up at the man in the hammock.

'I must rouse the cook,' he said to himself, with a smile. 'That fellow little thinks how useful he is in keeping up my spirits. The most inveterate croaker and grumbler in the world – and yet, according to his own account, the only cheerful man in the whole ship's company. John Want! John Want! Rouse up, there!'

A head rose slowly out of the bedclothes, covered with a red nightcap. A melancholy nose rested itself on the edge of the hammock. A voice, worthy of the nose, expressed its opinion of the Arctic climate, in these words:

'Lord! Lord! here's all my breath on my blanket. Icicles, if you please, sir, all round my mouth and all over my blanket. Every time I have snored, I've frozen something. When a man gets the cold into him to that extent that he ices his own bed, it can't last much longer. Never mind! *I* don't grumble.'

Crayford tapped the saucepan of bones impatiently. John Want lowered himself to the floor – grumbling all the way – by a rope attached to the rafters at his bedhead. Instead of approaching his superior officer and his saucepan, he hobbled, shivering, to the fireplace, and held his chin as close as he possibly could over the fire. Crayford looked after him.

'Halloo! what are you doing there?'

'Thawing my beard, sir.'

'Come here directly, and set to work on these bones.'

John Want remained immovably attached to the fireplace, holding something else over the fire. Crayford began to lose his temper.

'What the devil are you about now?'

'Thawing my watch, sir. It's been under my pillow all night, and the cold has stopped it. Cheerful, wholesome, bracing sort of climate to live in – isn't it, sir? Never mind! *I* don't grumble.'

'No, we all know that. Look here! Are these bones pounded small enough?'

John Want suddenly approached the lieutenant, and looked at him with an appearance of the deepest interest.

'You'll excuse me, sir,' he said; 'how very hollow your voice sounds this morning!'

'Never mind my voice. The bones! the bones!'

'Yes, sir – the bones. They'll take a trifle more pounding. I'll do my best with them, sir, for your sake.'

'What do you mean?'

John Want shook his head, and looked at Crayford with a dreary smile.

'I don't think I shall have the honour of making much more bone soup for you, sir. Do you think yourself you'll last long, sir? I don't, saving your presence. I think about another week or ten days will do for us all. Never mind! *I* don't grumble.'

He poured the bones into the mortar, and began to pound them – under protest. At the same moment a sailor appeared, entering from the inner hut.

'A message from Captain Ebsworth, sir.'

'Well?'

'The captain is worse than ever with his freezing pains, sir. He wants to see you immediately.'

'I will go at once. Rouse the doctor.'

Answering in those terms, Crayford returned to the inner hut, followed by the sailor. John Want shook his head again, and smiled more drearily than ever.

'Rouse the doctor?' he repeated. 'Suppose the doctor should be frozen? He hadn't a ha'porth of warmth in him last night, and his voice sounded like a whisper in a speaking-trumpet. Will the bones do now? Yes, the bones will do now. Into the saucepan with you,' cried John Want, suiting the action to the word, 'and flavour the hot water if you can! When I remember that I was once an apprentice at a pastry cook's – when I think of the gallons of turtle soup that this hand has stirred up in a jolly hot kitchen – and when I find myself mixing bones and hot water for soup, and turning into ice as fast as I can – if I wasn't of a cheerful disposition I should feel inclined to grumble. John Want! John Want! whatever had you done with your natural senses when you made up your mind to go to sea?'

A new voice hailed the cook, speaking from one of the bed-places in the side of the hut. It was the voice of Francis Aldersley.

'Who's that croaking over the fire?'

'Croaking?' repeated John Want, with the air of a man who considered himself the object of a gratuitous insult.

'Croaking? You don't find your own voice at all altered for the worse – do you, Mr Frank? I don't give *him*,' John proceeded, speaking confidentially to himself, 'more than six hours to last. He's one of your grumblers.'

'What are you doing there?' asked Frank.

'I'm making bone soup, sir, and wondering why I ever went to sea.'

'Well, and why did you go to sea?'

'I'm not certain, Mr Frank. Sometimes I think it was natural perversity; sometimes I think it was false pride at getting over seasickness; sometimes I think it was reading *Robinson Crusoe*, and books warning of me *not* to go to sea.'

Frank laughed. 'You're an odd fellow. What do you mean by false pride at getting over seasickness? Did you get over seasickness in some new way?'

John Want's dismal face brightened in spite of himself. Frank had recalled to the cook's memory one of the noteworthy passages in the cook's life.

'That's it, sir!' he said. 'If ever a man cured seasickness in a new way yet, I am that man – I got over it, Mr Frank, by dint of hard eating. I was a passenger on board a packet-boat, sir, when first I saw blue water. A nasty lopp of a sea came on at dinner-time, andI began to feel queer the moment the soup was put on the table. "Sick?" says the captain. "Rather, sir," says I. "Will you try my cure?" says the captain. "Certainly, sir," says I. "Is your heart in your mouth yet?" says the captain. "Not quite, sir," says I. "Mock-turtle soup?" says the captain, and helps me. I swallow a couple of spoonfuls, and turn as white as a sheet. The captain cocks his eye at me. "Go on deck, sir," says he; "get rid of the soup, and then come back to the cabin." I got rid of the soup, and came back to the cabin. "Cod's head and shoulders," says the captain, and helps me.

"I can't stand it, sir," says I. "You must," says the captain, "because it's the cure." I crammed down a mouthful, and turned paler than ever. "Go on deck," says the captain. "Get rid of the cod's head, and come back to the cabin." Off I go, and back I come. "Boiled leg of mutton and trimmings," says the captain, and helps me. "No fat, sir," says I. "Fat's the cure," says the captain, and makes me eat it. "Lean's the cure," says the captain, and makes me eat it. "Steady?" says the captain. "Sick," says I. "Go on deck," says the captain; "get rid of the boiled leg of mutton and trimmings and come back to the cabin." Off I go, staggering – back I come, more dead than alive. "Devilled kidneys," says the captain. I shut my eyes, and got 'em down. "Cure's beginning," says the captain. "Mutton-chop and pickles." I shut my eyes, and got *them* down. "Broiled ham and cayenne pepper," says the captain. "Glass of stout and cranberry tart. Want to go on deck again?" "No, sir," says I. "Cure's done," says the captain.

'Never you give in to your stomach, and your stomach will end in giving in to you.'

Having stated the moral purpose of his story in those unanswerable words, John Want took himself and his saucepan into the kitchen. A moment later, Crayford returned to the hut and astonished Frank Aldersley by an unexpected question.

'Have you anything in your berth, Frank, that you set a value on?'

'Nothing that I set the smallest value on – when I am out of it,' he replied. 'What does your question mean?'

'We are almost as short of fuel as we are of provisions,' Crayford proceeded. 'Your berth will make good firing. I have directed Bateson to be here in ten minutes with his axe.'

'Very attentive and considerate on your part,' said Frank.

'What is to become of me, if you please, when Bateson has chopped my bed into firewood?'

'Can't you guess?'

'I suppose the cold has stupefied me. The riddle is beyond my reading. Suppose you give me a hint?'

'Certainly. There will be beds to spare soon – there is to be a change at last in our wretched lives here. Do you see it now?'

Frank's eyes sparkled. He sprang out of his berth, and waved his fur cap in triumph.

'See it?' he exclaimed; 'of course I do! The exploring party is to start at last. Do I go with the expedition?'

'It is not very long since you were in the doctor's hands, Frank,' said Crayford, kindly. 'I doubt if you are strong enough yet to make one of the exploring party.'

'Strong enough or not,' returned Frank, 'any risk is better than pining and perishing here. Put me down, Crayford, among those who volunteer to go.'

'Volunteers will not be accepted in this case,' said Crayford. 'Captain Helding and Captain Ebsworth see serious objections, as we are situated, to that method of proceeding.'

'Do they mean to keep the appointments in their own hands?' asked Frank. 'I for one object to that.'

'Wait a little,' said Crayford. 'You were playing backgammon the other day with one of the officers. Does the board belong to him or to you?'

'It belongs to me. I have got it in my locker here. What do you want with it?'

'I want the dice and the box for casting lots. The captains have arranged – most wisely, as I think – that chance shall decide among us who goes with the expedition and who stays behind in the huts. The officers and crew of the *Wanderer* will be here in a few minutes to cast the lots. Neither you nor anyone can object to that way of deciding among us. Officers and men alike take their chance together. Nobody can grumble.'

'I am quite satisfied,' said Frank. 'But I know of one man among the officers who is sure to make objections.'

'Who is the man?'

'You know him well enough, too. The "Bear of the Expeditions" – Richard Wardour.'

'Frank! Frank! you have a bad habit of letting your tongue run away with you. Don't repeat that stupid nickname when you talk of my good friend, Richard Wardour.'

'Your good friend? Crayford! Your liking for that man amazes me.'

Crayford laid his hand kindly on Frank's shoulder. Of all the officers of the *Sea-mew*, Crayford's favourite was Frank.

'Why should it amaze you?' he asked. 'What opportunities have you had of judging? You and Wardour have always belonged to different ships. I have never seen you in Wardour's society for five minutes together. How can *you* form a fair estimate of his character?'

'I take the general estimate of his character,' Frank answered. 'He has got his nickname because he is the most unpopular man in his ship. Nobody likes him – there must be some reason for that.'

'There is only one reason for it,' Crayford rejoined. 'Nobody understands Richard Wardour. I am not talking at random. Remember, I sailed from England with him in the *Wanderer*; and I was only transferred to the *Sea-mew* long after we were locked up in the ice. I was Richard Wardour's companion on board ship for months, and I learnt there to do him justice. Under all his outward defects, I tell you, there beats a great and generous heart. Suspend your opinion, my lad, until you know my friend as well as I do. No more of this now. Give me the dice and the box.'

Frank opened his locker. At the same moment the silence of the snowy waste outside was broken by a shouting of voices hailing the hut – '*Sea-mew*, ahoy!'

CHAPTER EIGHT

The sailor on watch opened the outer door. There, plodding over the ghastly white snow, were the officers of the *Wanderer* approaching the hut. There, scattered under the merciless black sky, were the crew, with the dogs and the sledges, waiting the word which was to start them on their perilous and doubtful journey.

Captain Helding of the *Wanderer*, accompanied by his officers, entered the hut, in high spirits at the prospect of a change. Behind them, lounging in slowly by himself, was a dark, sullen, heavy-browed man. He neither spoke, nor offered his hand to anybody: he was the one person present who seemed to be perfectly indifferent to the fate in store for him. This was the man whom his brother officers had nicknamed the Bear of the Expedition. In other words – Richard Wardour.

Crayford advanced to welcome Captain Helding. Frank, remembering the friendly reproof which he had just received, passed over the other officers of the *Wanderer*, and made a special effort to be civil to Crayford's friend.

'Good morning, Mr Wardour,' he said. 'We may congratulate each other on the chance of leaving this horrible place.'

'*You* may think it horrible,' Wardour retorted; 'I like it.'

'Like it? Good Heavens! why?'

'Because there are no women here.'

Frank turned to his brother officers, without making any further advances in the direction of Richard Wardour. The Bear of the Expedition was more unapproachable than ever.

In the meantime, the hut had become thronged by the able-bodied officers and men of the two ships. Captain Helding, standing in the midst of them, with Crayford by his side, proceeded to explain the purpose of the contemplated expedition to the audience which surrounded him.

He began in these words:

'Brother officers and men of the *Wanderer* and *Sea-mew*, it is my duty to tell you, very briefly, the reasons which have decided Captain Ebsworth and myself on dispatching an exploring party in search of help. Without recalling all the hardships we have suffered for the last two years – the destruction, first of one of our ships, then of the other; the death of some of our bravest and best companions; the vain battles we have been fighting with the ice and snow, and boundless desolation of these inhospitable regions – without dwelling on these things, it is my duty to remind you that this, the last place in which we have taken refuge, is far beyond the track of any previous expedition, and that consequently our chance of being discovered by any rescuing parties that may be sent to look after us is, to say the least of it, a chance of the most uncertain kind. You all agree with me, gentlemen, so far?'

The officers (with the exception of Wardour, who stood apart in sullen silence) all agreed, so far.

The captain went on.

'It is therefore urgently necessary that we should make another, and probably a last, effort to extricate ourselves. The winter is not far off, game is getting scarcer and scarcer, our stock of provisions is running low, and the sick – especially, I am sorry to say, the sick in the *Wanderer*'s hut – are increasing in number day by day. We must look to our own lives, and to the lives of those who are dependent on us; and we have no time to lose.'

The officers echoed the words cheerfully.

'Right! right! No time to lose.'

Captain Helding resumed:

'The plan proposed is that a detachment of the able-bodied officers and men among us should set forth this very day, and make another effort to reach the nearest inhabited settlements, from which help and provisions may be dispatched to those who remain here. The new direction to be taken, and the various precautions to be adopted, are all drawn out ready. The only question now before us is who is to stop here, and who is to undertake the journey?'

The officers answered the question with one accord – 'Volunteers!'

The men echoed their officers. 'Ay, ay, volunteers.'

Wardour still preserved his sullen silence. Crayford noticed him standing apart from the rest, and appealed to him personally.

'Do you say nothing?' he asked.

'Nothing,' Wardour answered. 'Go or stay, it's all one to me.'

'I hope you don't really mean that?' said Crayford.

'I do.'

'I am sorry to hear it, Wardour.'

Captain Helding answered the general suggestion in favour of volunteering by a question which instantly checked the rising enthusiasm of the meeting.

'Well,' he said, 'suppose we say volunteers. Who volunteers to stop in the huts?'

There was a dead silence. The officers and men looked at each other confusedly. The captain continued:

'You see we can't settle it by volunteering. You all want to go. Every man among us who has the use of his limbs naturally wants to go. But what is to become of those who have not got the use of their limbs? Some of us must stay here, and take care of the sick.'

Everybody admitted that this was true.

'So we get back again,' said the captain, 'to the old question – who among the able-bodied is to go? and who is to stay? Captain Ebsworth says, and I say, let chance decide it. Here are dice. The numbers run as high as twelve – double sixes. All who throw under six, stay; all who throw over six, go. Officers of the *Wanderer* and the *Sea-mew*, do you agree to that way of meeting the difficulty?'

All the officers agreed, with the one exception of Wardour, who still kept silence.

'Men of the *Wanderer* and *Sea-mew*, your officers agree to cast lots. Do you agree too?'

The men agreed without a dissentient voice. Crayford handed the box and the dice to Captain Helding.

'You throw first, sir. Under six, stay. Over six, go.'

Captain Helding cast the dice, the top of the cask serving for a table. He threw seven.

'Go,' said Crayford. 'I congratulate you, sir. Now for my own chance.' He cast the dice in his turn. 'Three! Stay! Ah, well! well! if I can do my duty, and be of use to others, what does it matter whether I go or stay? Wardour, you are next, in the absence of your first lieutenant.'

Wardour prepared to cast, without shaking the dice.

'Shake the box, man!' cried Crayford. 'Give yourself a chance of luck!'

Wardour persisted in letting the dice fall out carelessly, just as they lay in the box.

'Not I!' he muttered to himself. 'I've done with luck.' Saying those words, he threw down the empty box, and seated himself on the nearest chest, without looking to see how the dice had fallen.

Crayford examined them. 'Six!' he exclaimed. 'There! you have a second chance, in spite of yourself. You are neither under nor over – you throw again.'

'Bah!' growled the Bear. 'It's not worth the trouble of getting up for. Somebody else throw for me.' He suddenly looked at Frank. 'You! you have got what the women call a lucky face.'

Frank appealed to Crayford. 'Shall I?'

'Yes, if he wishes it,' said Crayford.

Frank cast the dice. 'Two! He stays! Wardour, I am sorry I have thrown against you.'

'Go or stay,' reiterated Wardour, 'it's all one to me. You will be luckier, young one, when you cast for yourself.'

Frank cast for himself.

'Eight. Hurrah! I go!'

'What did I tell you?' said Wardour. 'The chance was yours. You have thrived on my ill luck.'

He rose, as he spoke, to leave the hut. Crayford stopped him.

'Have you anything particular to do, Richard?'

'What has anybody to do here?'

'Wait a little, then. I want to speak to you when this business is over.'

'Are you going to give me any more good advice?'

'Don't look at me in that sour way, Richard. I am going to ask you a question about something which concerns yourself.'

Wardour yielded without a word more. He returned to his chest, and cynically composed himself to slumber. The casting of the lots went on rapidly among the officers and men. In another half hour chance had decided the question of 'go' or 'stay' for all alike. The men left the hut. The officers entered the inner apartment for a last conference with the bedridden captain of the *Sea-mew*. Wardour and Crayford were left together, alone.

CHAPTER NINE

Crayford touched his friend on the shoulder to rouse him. Wardour looked up, impatiently, with a frown.

'I was just asleep,' he said. 'Why do you wake me?'

'Look round you, Richard. We are alone.'

'Well – and what of that?'

'I wish to speak to you privately – and this is my opportunity. You have disappointed and surprised me today. Why did you say it was all one to you whether you went or stayed? Why are you the only man among us who seems to be perfectly indifferent whether we are rescued or not?'

'Can a man always give a reason for what is strange in his manner or his words?' Wardour retorted.

'He can try,' said Crayford, quietly – 'when his friend asks him.'

Wardour's manner softened.

'That's true,' he said. 'I *will* try. Do you remember the first night at sea when we sailed from England in the *Wanderer*?'

'As well as if it was yesterday.'

'A calm, still night,' the other went on, thoughtfully. 'No clouds, no stars. Nothing in the sky but the broad moon, and hardly a ripple to break the path of light she made in the quiet water. Mine was the middle watch that night. You came on deck, and found me alone –'

He stopped. Crayford took his hand, and finished the sentence for him.

'Alone – and in tears.'

'The last I shall ever shed,' Wardour added, bitterly.

'Don't say that! There are times when a man is to be pitied indeed if he can shed no tears. Go on, Richard.'

Wardour proceeded – still following the old recollections,

still preserving his gentler tones.

'I should have quarrelled with any other man who had surprised me at that moment,' he said. 'There was something, I suppose, in your voice when you asked my pardon for disturbing me that softened my heart. I told you I had met with a disappointment which had broken me for life. There was no need to explain further. The only hopeless wretchedness in this world is the wretchedness that women cause.'

'And the only unalloyed happiness,' said Crayford, 'the happiness that women bring.'

'That may be your experience of them,' Wardour answered; 'mine is different. All the devotion, the patience, the humility, the worship that there is in man, I laid at the feet of a woman. She accepted the offering as women do – accepted it, easily, gracefully, unfeelingly – accepted it as a matter of course. I left England to win a high place in my profession before I dared to win *her*. I braved danger, and faced death. I staked my life in the fever swamps of Africa to gain the promotion that I only desired for her sake – and gained it. I came back to give her all, and to ask nothing in return, but to rest my weary heart in the sunshine of her smile. And her own lips – the lips I had kissed at parting – told me that another man had robbed me of her. I spoke but few words when I heard that confession, and left her forever. "The time may come," I told her, "when I shall forgive *you*. But the man who has robbed me of you shall rue the day when you and he first met." Don't ask me who he was! I have yet to discover him. The treachery had been kept secret; nobody could tell me where to find him; nobody could tell me who he was. What did it matter? When I had lived out the first agony, I could rely on myself – I could be patient, and bide my time.'

'Your time? What time?'

'The time when I and that man shall meet face to face. I knew it then; I know it now – it was written on my heart then, it is written on my heart now – we two shall meet and know each other! With that conviction strong within me, I volunteered for this service, as I would have volunteered for anything that set work and hardship and danger, like ramparts, between my misery and me. With that conviction strong within me still, I tell you it is no matter whether I stay here with the sick, or go hence with the strong. I shall live till I have met that man! There is a day of reckoning appointed between us. Here in the freezing cold, or away in the deadly heat; in battle or in shipwreck; in the face of starvation; under the shadow of pestilence – I, though hundreds are falling round me, I shall live! live for the coming of one day! live for the meeting with one man!'

He stopped, trembling, body and soul, under the hold that his own terrible superstition had fastened on him. Crayford drew back in silent horror. Wardour noticed the action – he resented it – he appealed, in defence of his one cherished conviction, to Crayford's own experience of him.

'Look at me!' he cried. 'Look how I have lived and thrived, with the heartache gnawing at me at home, and the winds of the icy north whistling round me here! I am the strongest man among you. Why? I have fought through hardships that have laid the best-seasoned men of all our party on their backs. Why? What have *I* done that my life should throb as bravely through every vein in my body at this minute, and in this deadly place, as ever it did in the wholesome breezes of home? What am I preserved for? I tell you again, for the coming of one day – for the meeting with one man.'

He paused once more. This time Crayford spoke.

'Richard!' he said, 'since we first met, I have believed in

your better nature, against all outward appearance. I have believed in you, firmly, truly, as your brother might. You are putting that belief to a hard test. If your enemy had told me that you had ever talked as you talk now, that you had ever looked as you look now, I would have turned my back on him as the utterer of a vile calumny against a just, a brave, an upright man. Oh! my friend, my friend, if ever I have deserved well of you, put away these thoughts from your heart! Face me again, with the stainless look of a man who has trampled under his feet the bloody superstitions of revenge, and knows them no more! Never, never, let the time come when I cannot offer you my hand as I offer it now, to the man I can still admire – to the brother I can still love!'

The heart that no other voice could touch felt that appeal. The fierce eyes, the hard voice, softened under Crayford's influence. Richard Wardour's head sank on his breast.

'You are kinder to me than I deserve,' he said. 'Be kinder still, and forget what I have been talking about. No! no more about me; I am not worth it. We'll change the subject, and never go back to it again. Let's do something. Work, Crayford – that's the true elixir of our life! Work, that stretches the muscles and sets the blood a-glowing. Work, that tires the body and rests the mind. Is there nothing in hand that I can do? Nothing to cut? Nothing to carry?'

The door opened as he put the question. Bateson – appointed to chop Frank's bed-place into firing – appeared punctually with his axe. Wardour, without a word of warning, snatched the axe out of the man's hand.

'What was this wanted for?' he asked.

'To cut up Mr Aldersley's berth there into firing, sir.'

'I'll do it for you! I'll have it down in no time!' He turned to Crayford. 'You needn't be afraid about me, old friend. I am going to do the right thing. I am going to tire my body and rest my mind.'

The evil spirit in him was plainly subdued – for the time, at least. Crayford took his hand in silence; and then (followed by Bateson) left him to his work.

CHAPTER TEN

Axe in hand, Wardour approached Frank's bed-place.

'If I could only cut the thoughts out of me,' he said to himself, 'as I am going to cut the billets out of this wood!' He attacked the bed-place with the axe, like a man who well knew the use of his instrument. 'Oh me!' he thought, sadly, 'if I had only been born a carpenter instead of a gentleman! A good axe, Master Bateson – I wonder where you got it? Something like a grip, my man, on this handle. Poor Crayford! His words stick in my throat. A fine fellow! a noble fellow! No use thinking, no use regretting; what is said, is said. Work! work! work!'

Plank after plank fell out on the floor. He laughed over the easy task of destruction. 'Aha! young Aldersley! It doesn't take much to demolish your bed-place. I'll have it down! I would have the whole hut down, if they would only give me the chance of chopping at it!'

A long strip of wood fell to his axe – long enough to require cutting in two. He turned it, and stooped over it. Something caught his eye – letters carved in the wood. He looked closer. The letters were very faintly and badly cut. He could only make out the first three of them; and even of those he was not quite certain. They looked like C L A – if they looked like anything. He threw down the strip of wood irritably.

'Damn the fellow (whoever he is) who cut this! Why should he carve *that* name, of all the names in the world?'

He paused, considering – then determined to go on again with his self-imposed labour. He was ashamed of his own outburst. He looked eagerly for the axe. 'Work, work! Nothing for it but work.' He found the axe, and went on again.

He cut out another plank.

He stopped, and looked at it suspiciously.

There was carving again, on this plank. The letters F and A appeared on it.

He put down the axe. There were vague misgivings in him which he was not able to realise. The state of his own mind was fast becoming a puzzle to him.

'More carving,' he said to himself. 'That's the way these young idlers employ their long hours. F.A.? Those must be *his* initials – Frank Aldersley. Who carved the letters on the other plank? Frank Aldersley, too?'

He turned the piece of wood in his hand nearer to the light, and looked lower down it. More carving again, lower down! Under the initials F.A. were two more letters – C.B.

'C.B.?' he repeated to himself. 'His sweetheart's initials, I suppose? Of course – at his age – his sweetheart's initials.'

He paused once more. A spasm of inner pain showed the shadow of its mysterious passage, outwardly on his face.

'*Her* cipher is C.B.,' he said, in low, broken tones. 'C.B. – Clara Burnham.'

He waited, with the plank in his hand; repeating the name over and over again, as if it was a question he was putting to himself.

'Clara Burnham? Clara Burnham?'

He dropped the plank, and turned deadly pale in a moment. His eyes wandered furtively backwards and forwards between the strip of wood on the floor and the half-demolished berth. 'Oh, God! what has come to me now?' he said to himself, in a whisper. He snatched up the axe, with a strange cry – something between rage and terror. He tried – fiercely, desperately tried – to go on with his work. No! strong as he was, he could not use the axe. His hands were helpless; they trembled incessantly. He went to the fire; he held his hands over it. They still trembled incessantly; they infected the rest of him. He shuddered all over. He knew fear. His own thoughts terrified him.

'Crayford!' he cried out. 'Crayford! come here, and let's go hunting.'

No friendly voice answered him. No friendly face showed itself at the door.

An interval passed; and there came over him another change. He recovered his self-possession almost as suddenly as he had lost it. A smile – a horrid, deforming, unnatural smile – spread slowly, stealthily, devilishly over his face. He left the fire; he put the axe away softly in a corner; he sat down in his old place, deliberately self-abandoned to a frenzy of vindictive joy. He had found the man! There, at the end of the world – there, at the last fight of the Arctic voyagers against starvation and death, he had found the man!

The minutes passed.

He became conscious, all of a sudden, of a freezing stream of air pouring into the room.

He turned, and saw Crayford opening the door of the hut. A man was behind him. Wardour rose eagerly, and looked over Crayford's shoulder.

Was it – could it be – the man who had carved the letters on the plank? Yes! Frank Aldersley!

CHAPTER ELEVEN

'Still at work!' Crayford exclaimed, looking at the half-demolished bed-place. 'Give yourself a little rest, Richard. The exploring party is ready to start. If you wish to take leave of your brother officers before they go, you have no time to lose.'

He checked himself there, looking Wardour full in the face.

'Good heavens!' he cried, 'how pale you are! Has anything happened?'

Frank – searching in his locker for articles of clothing which he might require on the journey – looked round. He was startled, as Crayford had been startled, by the sudden change in Wardour since they had last seen him.

'Are you ill?' he asked. 'I hear you have been doing Bateson's work for him. Have you hurt yourself?'

Wardour suddenly moved his head, so as to hide his face from both Crayford and Frank. He took out his handkerchief, and wound it clumsily round his left hand.

'Yes,' he said; 'I hurt myself with the axe. It's nothing. Never mind. Pain always has a curious effect on me. I tell you it's nothing! Don't notice it!'

He turned his face towards them again as suddenly as he had turned it away. He advanced a few steps, and addressed himself with an uneasy familiarity to Frank.

'I didn't answer you civilly when you spoke to me some little time since. I mean when I first came in here along with the rest of them. I apologise. Shake hands! How are you? Ready for the march?'

Frank met the oddly abrupt advance which had been made to him with perfect good humour.

'I am glad to be friends with you, Mr Wardour. I wish I was as well seasoned to fatigue as you are.'

Wardour burst into a hard, joyless, unnatural laugh.

'Not strong, eh? You don't look it. The dice had better have sent me away, and kept you here. I never felt in better condition in my life.' He paused and added, with his eye on Frank and with a strong emphasis on the words: 'We men of Kent are made of tough material.'

Frank advanced a step on his side, with a new interest in Richard Wardour.

'You come from Kent?' he said.

'Yes. From east Kent.' He waited a little once more, and looked hard at Frank. 'Do you know that part of the country?' he asked.

'I ought to know something about east Kent,' Frank answered. 'Some dear friends of mine once lived there.'

'Friends of yours?' Wardour repeated. 'One of the county families, I suppose?'

As he put the question, he abruptly looked over his shoulder. He was standing between Crayford and Frank. Crayford, taking no part in the conversation, had been watching him, and listening to him more and more attentively as that conversation went on. Within the last moment or two Wardour had become instinctively conscious of this. He resented Crayford's conduct with needless irritability.

'Why are you staring at me?' he asked.

'Why are you looking unlike yourself?' Crayford answered, quietly.

Wardour made no reply. He renewed the conversation with Frank.

'One of the county families?' he resumed. 'The Winterbys of Yew Grange, I dare say?'

'No,' said Frank; 'but friends of the Winterbys, very likely. The Burnhams.'

Desperately as he struggled to maintain it, Wardour's self-control failed him. He started violently. The clumsily wound handkerchief fell off his hand. Still looking at him attentively, Crayford picked it up.

'There is your handkerchief, Richard,' he said. 'Strange!'

'What is strange?'

'You told us you had hurt yourself with the axe –'

'Well?'

'There is no blood on your handkerchief.'

Wardour snatched the handkerchief out of Crayford's hand, and, turning away, approached the outer door of the hut. 'No blood on the handkerchief,' he said to himself. 'There may be a stain or two when Crayford sees it again.' He stopped within a few paces of the door, and spoke to Crayford. 'You recommended me to take leave of my brother officers before it was too late,' he said. 'I am going to follow your advice.'

The door was opened from the outer side as he laid his hand on the lock. One of the quartermasters of the *Wanderer* entered the hut.

'Is Captain Helding here, sir?' he asked, addressing himself to Wardour.

Wardour pointed to Crayford.

'The lieutenant will tell you,' he said.

Crayford advanced and questioned the quartermaster. 'What do you want with Captain Helding?' he asked.

'I have a report to make, sir. There has been an accident on the ice.'

'To one of your men?'

'No, sir. To one of our officers.'

Wardour, on the point of going out, paused when the quartermaster made that reply. For a moment he considered with himself. Then he walked slowly back to the part of the room in which Frank was standing. Crayford, directing the quartermaster, pointed to the arched doorway in the side of the hut.

'I am sorry to hear of the accident,' he said. 'You will find Captain Helding in that room.'

For the second time, with singular persistency, Wardour renewed the conversation with Frank.

'So you knew the Burnhams?' he said. 'What became of Clara when her father died?'

Frank's face flushed angrily on the instant.

'Clara!' he repeated. 'What authorises you to speak of Miss Burnham in that familiar manner?'

Wardour seized the opportunity of quarrelling with him.

'What right have you to ask?' he retorted, coarsely.

Frank's blood was up. He forgot his promise to Clara to keep their engagement secret – he forgot everything but the unbridled insolence of Wardour's language and manner.

'A right which I insist on your respecting,' he answered. 'The right of being engaged to marry her.'

Crayford's steady eyes were still on the watch, and Wardour felt them on him. A little more and Crayford might openly interfere. Even Wardour recognised for once the necessity of controlling his temper, cost him what it might. He made his apologies, with overstrained politeness, to Frank.

'Impossible to dispute such a right as yours,' he said. 'Perhaps you will excuse me when you know that I am one of Miss Burnham's old friends. My father and her father were neighbours. We have always met like brother and sister –'

Frank generously stopped the apology there.

'Say no more,' he interposed. 'I was in the wrong – I lost my temper. Pray forgive me.'

Wardour looked at him with a strange, reluctant interest

while he was speaking. Wardour asked an extraordinary question when he had done.

'Is she very fond of you?'

Frank burst out laughing.

'My dear fellow,' he said, 'come to our wedding, and judge for yourself.'

'Come to your wedding?' As he repeated the words Wardour stole one glance at Frank which Frank (employed in buckling his knapsack) failed to see. Crayford noticed it, and Crayford's blood ran cold. Comparing the words which Wardour had spoken to him while they were alone together with the words that had just passed in his presence, he could draw but one conclusion. The woman whom Wardour had loved and lost was Clara Burnham. The man who had robbed him of her was Frank Aldersley. And Wardour had discovered it in the interval since they had last met. 'Thank God!' thought Crayford, 'the dice have parted them! Frank goes with the expedition, and Wardour stays behind with me.'

The reflection had barely occurred to him – Frank's thoughtless invitation to Wardour had just passed his lips – when the canvas screen over the doorway was drawn aside. Captain Helding and the officers who were to leave with the exploring party returned to the main room on their way out. Seeing Crayford, Captain Helding stopped to speak to him.

'I have a casualty to report,' said the captain, 'which diminishes our numbers by one. My second lieutenant, who was to have joined the exploring party, has had a fall on the ice. Judging by what the quartermaster tells me, I am afraid the poor fellow has broken his leg.'

'I will supply his place,' cried a voice at the other end of the hut. Everybody looked round. The man who had spoken was Richard Wardour.

Crayford instantly interfered – so vehemently as to astonish all who knew him.

'No!' he said. 'Not you, Richard! not you!'

'Why not?' Wardour asked, sternly.

'Why not, indeed?' added Captain Helding. 'Wardour is the very man to be useful on a long march. He is in perfect health, and he is the best shot among us. I was on the point of proposing him myself.'

Crayford failed to show his customary respect for his superior officer. He openly disputed the captain's conclusion.

'Wardour has no right to volunteer,' he rejoined. 'It has been settled, Captain Helding, that chance shall decide who is to go and who is to stay.'

'And chance *has* decided it,' cried Wardour. 'Do you think we are going to cast the dice again, and give an officer of the *Sea-mew* a chance of replacing an officer of the *Wanderer*? There is a vacancy in our party, not in yours; and we claim the right of filling it as we please. I volunteer, and my captain backs me. Whose authority is to keep me here after that?'

'Gently, Wardour,' said Captain Helding. 'A man who is in the right can afford to speak with moderation.' He turned to Crayford. 'You must admit yourself,' he continued, 'that Wardour is right this time. The missing man belongs to my command, and in common justice one of my officers ought to supply his place.'

It was impossible to dispute the matter further. The dullest man present could see that the captain's reply was unanswerable. In sheer despair, Crayford took Frank's arm and led him aside a few steps. The last chance left of parting the two men was the chance of appealing to Frank.

'My dear boy,' he began, 'I want to say one friendly word to you on the subject of your health. I have already, if you remember, expressed my doubts whether you are strong enough to make one of an exploring party. I feel those doubts more strongly than ever at this moment. Will you take the advice of a friend who wishes you well?'

Wardour had followed Crayford. Wardour roughly interposed before Frank could reply.

'Let him alone!'

Crayford paid no heed to the interruption. He was too earnestly bent on withdrawing Frank from the expedition to notice anything that was said or done by the persons about him.

'Don't, pray don't risk hardships which you are unfit to bear!' he went on, entreatingly. 'Your place can be easily filled. Change your mind, Frank. Stay here with me.'

Again Wardour interfered. Again he called out, 'Leave him alone!' more roughly than ever. Still deaf and blind to every consideration but one, Crayford pressed his entreaties on Frank.

'You owned yourself just now that you were not well seasoned to fatigue,' he persisted. 'You feel – you *must* feel – how weak that last illness has left you? You know – I am sure you know – how unfit you are to brave exposure to cold, and long marches over the snow.'

Irritated beyond endurance by Crayford's obstinacy; seeing, or thinking he saw, signs of yielding in Frank's face, Wardour so far forgot himself as to seize Crayford by the arm and attempt to drag him away from Frank. Crayford turned and looked at him.

'Richard,' he said, very quietly, 'you are not yourself. I pity you. Drop your hand.'

Wardour relaxed his hold, with something of the sullen submission of a wild animal to its keeper. The momentary silence which followed gave Frank an opportunity of speaking at last.

'I am gratefully sensible, Crayford,' he began, 'of the interest which you take in me –'

'And you will follow my advice?' Crayford interposed, eagerly.

'My mind is made up, old friend,' Frank answered, firmly and sadly. 'Forgive me for disappointing you. I am appointed to the expedition. With the expedition I go.' He moved nearer to Wardour. In his innocence of all suspicion he clapped Wardour heartily on the shoulder. 'When I feel the fatigue,' said poor simple Frank, 'you will help me, comrade – won't you? Come along!'

Wardour snatched his gun out of the hands of the sailor who was carrying it for him. His dark face became suddenly irradiated with a terrible joy.

'Come!' he cried. 'Over the snow and over the ice! Come! where no human footsteps have ever trodden, and where no human trace is ever left.'

Blindly, instinctively, Crayford made an effort to part them. His brother officers, standing near, pulled him back. They looked at each other anxiously. The merciless cold, striking its victims in various ways, had struck in some instances at their reason first. Everybody loved Crayford. Was he, too, going on the dark way that others had taken before him? They forced him to seat himself on one of the lockers. 'Steady, old fellow!' they said kindly – 'steady!' Crayford yielded, writhing inwardly under the sense of his own helplessness. What in God's name could he do? Could he denounce Wardour to Captain Helding on bare suspicion – without so much as the shadow of a proof to justify what he said? The captain would decline to insult one of his officers by even mentioning the monstrous accusation to him. The captain would conclude, as others had already concluded, that Crayford's mind was giving way under stress of cold and privation. No hope – literally, no hope now, but in the numbers of the expedition. Officers and men, they all liked Frank. As long as they could stir hand or foot, they would help him on the way – they would see that no harm came to him.

The word of command was given; the door was thrown open; the hut emptied rapidly. Over the merciless white snow – under the merciless black sky – the exploring party began to move. The sick and helpless men, whose last hope of rescue centred in their departing messmates, cheered faintly. Some few whose days were numbered sobbed and cried like women. Frank's voice faltered as he turned back at the door to say his last words to the friend who had been a father to him.

'God bless you, Crayford!'

Crayford broke away from the officers near him; and, hurrying forwards, seized Frank by both hands. Crayford held him as if he would never let him go.

'God preserve you, Frank! I would give all I have in the world to be with you. Goodbye! Goodbye!'

Frank waved his hand – dashed away the tears that were gathering in his eyes – and hurried out. Crayford called after him, the last, the only warning that he could give:

'While you can stand, keep with the main body, Frank!'

Wardour, waiting till the last – Wardour, following Frank through the snowdrift – stopped, stepped back, and answered Crayford at the door:

'While he can stand, he keeps with me.'

CHAPTER TWELVE

Alone! alone on the Frozen Deep!

The Arctic sun is rising dimly in the dreary sky. The beams of the cold northern moon, mingling strangely with the dawning light, clothe the snowy plains in hues of livid grey. An ice field on the far horizon is moving slowly southward in the spectral light. Nearer, a stream of open water rolls its slow black waves past the edges of the ice. Nearer still, following the drift, an iceberg rears its crags and pinnacles to the sky; here, glittering in the moonbeams; there, looming dim and ghost-like in the ashy light.

Midway on the long sweep of the lower slope of the iceberg, what objects rise, and break the desolate monotony of the scene? In this awful solitude, can signs appear which tell of human life? Yes! The black outline of a boat just shows itself, hauled up on the berg. In an ice cavern behind the boat the last red embers of a dying fire flicker from time to time over the figures of two men. One is seated, resting his back against the side of the cavern. The other lies prostrate, with his head on his comrade's knee. The first of these men is awake, and thinking. The second reclines, with his still white face turned up to the sky – sleeping or dead. Days and days since, these two have fallen behind on the march of the expedition of relief. Days and days since, these two have been given up by their weary and failing companions as doomed and lost. He who sits thinking is Richard Wardour. He who lies sleeping or dead is Frank Aldersley.

The iceberg drifts slowly, over the black water, through the ashy light. Minute by minute the dying fire sinks. Minute by minute the deathly cold creeps nearer and nearer to the lost men.

Richard Wardour rouses himself from his thoughts – looks at the still white face beneath him – and places his hand on Frank's heart. It still beats feebly. Give him his share of the food and fuel still stored in the boat, and Frank may live through it. Leave him neglected where he lies, and his death is a question of hours – perhaps minutes – who knows?

Richard Wardour lifts the sleeper's head and rests it against the cavern side. He goes to the boat, and returns with a billet of wood. He stoops to place the wood on the fire – and stops. Frank is dreaming, and murmuring in his dream. A woman's name passes his lips. Frank is in England again – at the ball – whispering to Clara the confession of his love.

Over Richard Wardour's face there passes the shadow of a deadly thought. He rises from the fire; he takes the wood back to the boat. His iron strength is shaken, but it still holds out. They are drifting nearer and nearer to the open sea. He can launch the boat without help; he can take the food and the fuel with him. The sleeper on the iceberg is the man who has robbed him of Clara – who has wrecked the hope and the happiness of his life. Leave the man in his sleep, and let him die!

So the tempter whispers. Richard Wardour tries his strength on the boat. It moves: he has got it under control. He stops, and looks round. Beyond him is the open sea. Beneath him is the man who has robbed him of Clara. The shadow of the deadly thought grows and darkens over his face. He waits with his hands on the boat – waits and thinks.

The iceberg drifts slowly, over the black water, through the ashy light. Minute by minute the dying fire sinks. Minute by minute the deathly cold creeps nearer to the sleeping man. And still Richard Wardour waits – waits and thinks.

CHAPTER THIRTEEN

The spring has come. The air of the April night just lifts the leaves of the sleeping flowers. The moon is queen in the cloudless and starless sky. The stillness of the midnight hour is abroad, over land and over sea.

In a villa on the westward shore of the Isle of Wight, the glass doors which lead from the drawing room to the garden are yet open. The shaded lamp yet burns on the table. A lady sits by the lamp, reading. From time to time she looks out into the garden, and sees the white-robed figure of a young girl pacing slowly to and fro in the soft brightness of the moonlight on the lawn. Sorrow and suspense have set their mark on the lady. Not rivals only, but friends who formerly admired her, agree now that she looks worn and aged. The more merciful judgement of others remarks, with equal truth, that her eyes, her hair, her simple grace and grandeur of movement have lost but little of their olden charms. The truth lies, as usual, between the two extremes. In spite of sorrow and suffering, Mrs Crayford is the beautiful Mrs Crayford still.

The delicious silence of the hour is softly disturbed by the voice of the younger lady in the garden.

'Go to the piano, Lucy. It is a night for music. Play something that is worthy of the night.'

Mrs Crayford looks round at the clock on the mantelpiece.

'My dear Clara, it is past twelve! Remember what the doctor told you. You ought to have been in bed an hour ago.'

'Half an hour, Lucy – give me half an hour more! Look at the moonlight on the sea. Is it possible to go to bed on such a night as this? Play something, Lucy – something spiritual and divine.'

Earnestly pleading with her friend, Clara advances towards

the window. She too has suffered under the wasting influences of suspense. Her face has lost its youthful freshness; no delicate flush of colour rises on it when she speaks. The soft grey eyes which won Frank's heart in the bygone time are sadly altered now. In repose, they have a dimmed and wearied look. In action, they are wild and restless, like eyes suddenly wakened from startling dreams. Robed in white – her soft brown hair hanging loosely over her shoulders – there is something weird and ghost-like in the girl, as she moves nearer and nearer to the window in the full light of the moon – pleading for music that shall be worthy of the mystery and the beauty of the night.

'Will you come in here if I play to you?' Mrs Crayford asks. 'It is a risk, my love, to be out so long in the night air.'

'No! no! I like it. Play – while I am out here looking at the sea. It quiets me; it comforts me; it does me good.'

She glides back, ghost-like, over the lawn. Mrs Crayford rises, and puts down the volume that she has been reading. It is a record of explorations in the Arctic seas. The time has gone by when the two lonely women could take an interest in subjects not connected with their own anxieties. Now, when hope is fast failing them – now, when their last news of the *Wanderer* and the *Sea-mew* is news that is more than two years old – they can read of nothing, they can think of nothing, but dangers and discoveries, losses and rescues in the terrible Polar seas.

Unwillingly, Mrs Crayford puts her book aside, and opens the piano – Mozart's 'Air in A, with Variations' lies open on the instrument. One after another she plays the lovely melodies, so simply, so purely beautiful, of that unpretending and unrivalled work. At the close of the ninth Variation (Clara's favourite), she pauses, and turns towards the garden.

'Shall I stop there?' she asks.

There is no answer. Has Clara wandered away out of hearing of the music that she loves – the music that harmonises so subtly with the tender beauty of the night? Mrs Crayford rises and advances to the window.

No! there is the white figure standing alone on the slope of the lawn – the head turned away from the house; the face looking out over the calm sea, whose gently rippling waters end in the dim line on the horizon which is the line of the Hampshire coast.

Mrs Crayford advances as far as the path before the window, and calls to her.

'Clara!'

Again there is no answer. The white figure still stands immovably in its place.

With signs of distress in her face, but with no appearance of alarm, Mrs Crayford returns to the room. Her own sad experience tells her what has happened. She summons the servants and directs them to wait in the drawing room until she calls to them. This done, she returns to the garden, and approaches the mysterious figure on the lawn.

Dead to the outer world, as if she lay already in her grave – insensible to touch, insensible to sound, motionless as stone, cold as stone – Clara stands on the moonlit lawn, facing the seaward view. Mrs Crayford waits at her side, patiently watching for the change which she knows is to come. 'Catalepsy' as some call it – 'hysteria' as others say – this alone is certain, the same interval always passes; the same change always appears.

It comes now. Not a change in her eyes; they still remain wide open, fixed and glassy. The first movement is a movement of her hands. They rise slowly from her side and waver in the air like the hands of a person groping in the dark. Another interval, and the movement spreads to her lips: they part and tremble. A few minutes more, and words begin to drop, one by one, from those parted lips – words spoken in a lost, vacant tone, as if she is talking in her sleep.

Mrs Crayford looks back at the house. Sad experience makes her suspicious of the servants' curiosity. Sad experience has long since warned her that the servants are not to be trusted within hearing of the wild words which Clara speaks in the trance. Has anyone of them ventured into the garden? No. They are out of hearing at the window, waiting for the signal which tells them that their help is needed. Turning towards Clara once more, Mrs Crayford hears the vacantly uttered words, falling faster and faster from her lips:

'Frank! Frank! Frank! Don't drop behind – don't trust Richard Wardour. While you can stand, keep with the other men, Frank!'

(The farewell warning of Crayford in the solitudes of the Frozen Deep, repeated by Clara in the garden of her English home!)

A moment of silence follows; and, in that moment, the vision has changed. She sees him on the iceberg now, at the mercy of the bitterest enemy he has on earth. She sees him drifting, over the black water, through the ashy light.

'Wake, Frank! wake and defend yourself! Richard Wardour knows that I love you – Richard Wardour's vengeance will take your life! Wake, Frank – wake! You are drifting to your death!' A low groan of horror bursts from her, sinister and terrible to hear.

'Drifting! drifting!' she whispers to herself – 'drifting to his death!'

Her glassy eyes suddenly soften – then close. A long

shudder runs through her. A faint flush shows itself on the deadly pallor of her face, and fades again. Her limbs fail her. She sinks into Mrs Crayford's arms.

The servants, answering the call for help, carry her into the house. They lay her insensible on her bed. After half an hour or more, her eyes open again – this time with the light of life in them – open, and rest languidly on the friend sitting by the bedside.

'I have had a dreadful dream,' she murmurs faintly. 'Am I ill, Lucy? I feel so weak.'

Even as she says the words, sleep – gentle, natural sleep – takes her suddenly, as it takes young children weary with their play. Though it is all over now, though no further watching is required, Mrs Crayford still keeps her place by the bedside, too anxious and too wakeful to retire to her own room.

On other occasions she is accustomed to dismiss from her mind the words which drop from Clara in the trance. This time the effort to dismiss them is beyond her power. The words haunt her. Vainly she recalls to memory all that the doctors have said to her, in speaking of Clara in the state of trance. 'What she vaguely dreads for the lost man whom she loves is mingled in her mind with what she is constantly reading, of trials, dangers, and escapes in the Arctic seas. The most startling things that she may say or do are all attributable to this cause, and may all be explained in this way.' So the doctors have spoken; and, thus far, Mrs Crayford has shared their view. It is only tonight that the girl's words ring in her ear with a strange prophetic sound in them. It is only tonight that she asks herself: 'Is Clara present, in the spirit, with our loved and lost ones in the lonely North? Can mortal vision see the dead and living in the solitudes of the Frozen Deep?'

CHAPTER FOURTEEN

The night had passed.

Far and near the garden view looked its gayest and brightest in the light of the noonday sun. The cheering sounds which tell of life and action were audible all round the villa. From the garden of the nearest house rose the voices of children at play. Along the road at the back sounded the roll of wheels, as carts and carriages passed at intervals. Out on the blue sea, the distant splash of the paddles, the distant thump of the engines, told from time to time of the passage of steamers, entering or leaving the strait between the island and the mainland. In the trees, the birds sang gaily among the rustling leaves. In the house, the women servants were laughing over some jest or story that cheered them at their work. It was a lively and pleasant time – a bright, enjoyable day.

The two ladies were out together; resting on a garden seat, after a walk round the grounds. They exchanged a few trivial words relating to the beauty of the day, and then said no more. Possessing the same consciousness of what she had seen in the trance which persons in general possess of what they have seen in a dream – believing in the vision as a supernatural revelation – Clara's worst forebodings were now, to her mind, realised as truths. Her last faint hope of ever seeing Frank again was now at an end. Intimate experience of her told Mrs Crayford what was passing in Clara's mind, and warned her that the attempt to reason and remonstrate would be little better than a voluntary waste of words and time. The disposition which she had herself felt on the previous night – to attach a superstitious importance to the words that Clara had spoken in the trance – had vanished with the return of the morning. Rest and reflection had quieted her mind, and had restored the composing influence of her sober sense. Sympathising with Clara in all besides, she had no sympathy, as they sat together in the pleasant sunshine, with Clara's gloomy despair of the future. She, who could still hope, had nothing to say to the sad companion who had done with hope. So the quiet minutes succeeded each other, and the two friends sat side by side in silence.

An hour passed, and the gate-bell of the villa rang.

They both started – they both knew the ring. It was the hour when the postman brought their newspapers from London. In past days, what hundreds on hundreds of times they had torn off the cover which enclosed the newspaper, and looked at the same column with the same weary mingling of hope and despair! There today – as it was yesterday; as it would be, if they lived, tomorrow – there was the servant with Lucy's newspaper and Clara's newspaper in his hand!

Would both of them do again today what both had done so often in the days that were gone?

No! Mrs Crayford removed the cover from her newspaper as usual.

Clara laid *her* newspaper aside, unopened, on the garden seat.

In silence, Mrs Crayford looked, where she always looked, at the column devoted to the latest intelligence from foreign parts. The instant her eye fell on the page she started with a loud cry of joy. The newspaper fell from her trembling hand. She caught Clara in her arms. 'Oh, my darling! my darling! news of them at last.'

Without answering, without the slightest change in look or manner, Clara took the newspaper from the ground, and read the top line in the column, printed in capital letters:

She waited, and looked at Mrs Crayford. 'Can you bear to hear it, Lucy,' she asked, 'if I read it aloud?' Mrs Crayford was too agitated to answer in words. She signed impatiently to Clara to go on.

Clara read the news which followed the heading in capital letters. Thus it ran:

> *The following intelligence, from St Johns, Newfoundland, has reached us for publication. The whaling vessel Blythewood is reported to have met with the surviving officers and men of the Expedition in Davis Strait. Many are stated to be dead, and some are supposed to be missing. The list of the saved, as collected by the people of the whaler, is not vouched for as being absolutely correct, the circumstances having been adverse to investigation. The vessel was pressed for time; and the members of the Expedition, all more or less suffering from exhaustion, were not in a position to give the necessary assistance to enquiry. Further particulars may be looked for by the next mail.*

The list of the survivors followed, beginning with the officers in the order of their rank. They both read the list together. The first name was Captain Helding; the second was Lieutenant Crayford.

There the wife's joy overpowered her. After a pause, she put her arm around Clara's waist, and spoke to her.

'Oh, my love!' she murmured, 'are you as happy as I am? Is Frank's name there too? The tears are in my eyes. Read for – I can't read for myself.'

The answer came, in still, sad tones:

'I have read as far as your husband's name. I have no

need to read further.'

Mrs Crayford dashed the tears from her eyes – steadied herself – and looked at the newspaper.

On the list of the survivors, the search was vain. Frank's name was not among them. On a second list, headed 'Dead or Missing', the first two names that appeared were:

FRANCIS ALDERSLEY

RICHARD WARDOUR

In speechless distress and dismay, Mrs Crayford looked at Clara. Had she force enough in her feeble health to sustain the shock that had fallen on her? Yes! she bore it with a strange unnatural resignation – she looked, she spoke, with the sad self-possession of despair.

'I was prepared for it,' she said. 'I saw them in the spirit last night. Richard Wardour has discovered the truth; and Frank has paid the penalty with his life – and I, I alone, am to blame.' She shuddered, and put her hand on her heart. 'We shall not be long parted, Lucy. I shall go to him. He will not return to me.'

Those words were spoken with a calm certainty of conviction that was terrible to hear. 'I have no more to say,' she added, after a moment, and rose to return to the house. Mrs Crayford caught her by the hand, and forced her to take her seat again.

'Don't look at me, don't speak to me, in that horrible manner!' she exclaimed. 'Clara! it is unworthy of a reasonable being, it is doubting the mercy of God, to say what you have just said. Look at the newspaper again. See! They tell you plainly that their information is not to be depended on – they warn you to wait for further particulars. The very words at the top of the list show how little they knew of the truth 'Dead *or* Missing!' On their own showing, it is quite as likely that Frank is missing as that Frank is dead. For all you know, the next mail may bring a letter from him. Are you listening to me?'

'Yes.'

'Can you deny what I say?'

'No.'

' "Yes!" "No!" Is that the way to answer me when I am so distressed and so anxious about you?'

'I am sorry I spoke as I did, Lucy. We look at some subjects in very different ways. I don't dispute, dear, that yours is the reasonable view.'

'You don't dispute?' retorted Mrs Crayford, warmly. 'No! you do what is worse – you believe in your own opinion; you persist in your own conclusion – with the newspaper before you! Do you, or do you not, believe the newspaper?'

'I believe in what I saw last night.'

'In what you saw last night! You, an educated woman, a clever woman, believing in a vision of your own fancy – a mere dream! I wonder you are not ashamed to acknowledge it!'

'Call it a dream if you like, Lucy. I have had other dreams at other times – and I have known them to be fulfilled.'

'Yes!' said Mrs Crayford. 'For once in a way they may have been fulfilled, by chance – and you notice it, and remember it, and pin your faith on it. Come, Clara, be honest! – What about the occasions when the chance has been against you, and your dreams have not been fulfilled? You superstitious people are all alike. You conveniently forget when your dreams and your presentiments prove false. For my sake, dear, if not for your own,' she continued, in gentler and tenderer tones, 'try to be more reasonable and more hopeful. Don't lose your trust in the future, and your trust in God. God, who has saved my husband, can save Frank. While there is doubt, there is hope. Don't embitter my happiness, Clara! Try to think as I think – if it is only to show that you love me.'

She put her arm round the girl's neck and kissed her. Clara returned the kiss; Clara answered, sadly and submissively:

'I do love you, Lucy. I *will* try.'

Having answered in those terms, she sighed to herself, and said no more. It would have been plain, only too plain, to far less observant eyes than Mrs Crayford's that no salutary impression had been produced on her. She had ceased to defend her own way of thinking, she spoke of it no more – but there was the terrible conviction of Frank's death at Wardour's hands rooted as firmly as ever in her mind! Discouraged and distressed, Mrs Crayford left her, and walked back towards the house.

CHAPTER FIFTEEN

At the drawing-room window of the villa there appeared a polite little man, with bright intelligent eyes, and cheerful sociable manners. Neatly dressed in professional black, he stood, self-proclaimed, a prosperous country doctor – successful and popular in a wide circle of patients and friends. As Mrs Crayford approached him, he stepped out briskly to meet her on the lawn, with both hands extended in courteous and cordial greeting.

'My dear madam, accept my heartfelt congratulations!' cried the doctor. 'I have seen the good news in the paper; and I could hardly feel more rejoiced than I do now if I had the honour of knowing Lieutenant Crayford personally. We mean to celebrate the occasion at home. I said to my wife before I came out, "A bottle of the old Madeira at dinner today, mind! – to drink the lieutenant's health; God bless him!" And how is our interesting patient? The news is not altogether what we could wish, so far as she is concerned. I felt a little anxious, to tell you the truth, about the effect of it; and I have paid my visit today before my usual time. Not that I take a gloomy view of the news myself. No! There is clearly a doubt about the correctness of the information, so far as Mr Aldersley is concerned – and that is a point, a great point in Mr Aldersley's favour. I give him the benefit of the doubt, as the lawyers say. Does Miss Burnham give him the benefit of the doubt too? I hardly dare hope it, I confess.'

'Miss Burnham has grieved and alarmed me,' Mrs Crayford answered. 'I was just thinking of sending for you when we met here.'

With those introductory words, she told the doctor exactly what had happened; repeating not only the conversation of that morning between Clara and herself, but also the words which had fallen from Clara in the trance of the past night.

The doctor listened attentively. Little by little, its easy smiling composure vanished from his face as Mrs Crayford went on, and left him completely transformed into a grave and thoughtful man.

'Let us go and look at her,' he said.

He seated himself by Clara's side, and carefully studied her face, with his hand on her pulse. There was no sympathy here between the dreamy mystical temperament of the patient and the downright practical character of the doctor. Clara secretly disliked her medical attendant. She submitted impatiently to the close investigation of which he made her the object. He questioned her – and she answered irritably. Advancing a step further (the doctor was not easily discouraged) he adverted to the news of the expedition, and took up the tone of remonstrance which had been already adopted by Mrs Crayford. Clara declined to discuss the question. She rose with formal politeness, and requested permission to return to the house. The doctor attempted no further resistance. 'By all means, Miss Burnham,' he answered, resignedly – having first cast a look at Mrs Crayford which said plainly, 'Stay here with me.' Clara bowed her acknowledgments in cold silence, and left them together. The doctor's bright eyes followed the girl's wasted, yet still graceful figure as it slowly receded from view, with an expression of grave anxiety which Mrs Crayford noticed with grave misgiving on her side. He said nothing until Clara had disappeared under the veranda which ran round the garden side of the house.

'I think you told me,' he began, 'that Miss Burnham has neither father nor mother living?'

'Yes. Miss Burnham is an orphan.'

'Has she any near relatives?'

'No. You may speak to me as her guardian and her friend. Are you alarmed about her?'

'I am seriously alarmed. It is only two days since I called here last, and I see a marked change in her for the worse – physically and morally, a change for the worse. Don't needlessly alarm yourself! The case is not, I trust, entirely beyond the reach of remedy. The great hope for us is the hope that Mr Aldersley may still be living. In that event, I should feel no misgivings about the future. Her marriage would make a healthy and a happy woman of her. But as things are, I own I dread that settled conviction in her mind that Mr Aldersley is dead, and that her own death is soon to follow. In her present state of health this idea (haunting her as it certainly will night and day) will have its influence on her body as well as on her mind. Unless we can check the mischief, her last reserves of strength will give way. If you wish for other advice, by all means send for it. You have my opinion.'

'I am quite satisfied with your opinion,' Mrs Crayford replied. 'For God's sake, tell me, what can we do?'

'We can try a complete change,' said the doctor. 'We can remove her at once from this place.'

'She will refuse to leave it,' Mrs Crayford rejoined. 'I have more than once proposed a change to her – and she always says no.'

The doctor paused for a moment, like a man collecting his thoughts.

'I heard something on my way here,' he proceeded, 'which suggests to my mind a method of meeting the difficulty that you have just mentioned. Unless I am entirely mistaken, Miss Burnham will not say no to the change that I have in view for her.'

'What is it?' asked Mrs Crayford, eagerly.

'Pardon me if I ask you a question, on my part, before I reply,' said the doctor. 'Are you fortunate enough to possess any interest at the Admiralty?'

'Certainly. My father is in the Secretary's office; and two of the Lords of the Admiralty are friends of his.'

'Excellent! Now I can speak out plainly with little fear of disappointing you. After what I have said, you will agree with me that the only change in Miss Burnham's life which will be of any use to her is a change that will alter the present tone of her mind on the subject of Mr Aldersley. Place her in a position to discover – not by reference to her own distempered fancies and visions, but by reference to actual evidence and actual fact – whether Mr Aldersley is, or is not, a living man; and there will be an end of the hysterical delusions which now threaten to fatally undermine her health. Even taking matters at their worst – even assuming that Mr Aldersley has died in the Arctic seas – it will be less injurious to her to discover this positively than to leave her mind to feed on its own morbid superstitions and speculations, for weeks and weeks together, while the next news from the expedition is on its way to England. In one word, I want you to be in a position, before the week is out, to put Miss Burnham's present conviction to a practical test. Suppose you could say to her, "We differ, my dear, about Mr Francis Aldersley. You declare, without the shadow of a reason for it, that he is certainly dead, and, worse still, that he has died by the act of one of his brother officers. I assert, on the authority of the newspaper, that nothing of the sort has happened, and that the chances are all in favour of his being still a living man. What do you say to crossing the Atlantic, and deciding which of us is right – you or I?" Do you think Miss Burnham will say no to that, Mrs Crayford?

If I know anything of human nature, she will seize the opportunity as a means of converting you to a belief in the Second Sight.'

'Good heavens, Doctor! Do you mean to tell me that we are to go to sea and meet the Arctic Expedition on its way home?'

'Admirably guessed, Mrs Crayford! That is exactly what I mean.'

'But how is it to be done?'

'I will tell you immediately. I mentioned – didn't I? – that I had heard something on my road to this house.'

'Yes.'

'Well, I met an old friend at my own gate, who walked with me a part of the way here. Last night my friend dined with the Admiral at Portsmouth. Among the guests there was a member of the ministry who had brought the news about the expedition with him from London. This gentleman told the company there was very little doubt that the Admiralty would immediately send out a steam-vessel to meet the rescued men on the shores of America and bring them home. Wait a little, Mrs Crayford! Nobody knows, as yet, under what rules and regulations the vessel will sail. Under somewhat similar circumstances, privileged people have been received as passengers, or rather as guests, in Her Majesty's ships – and what has been conceded on former occasions may, by bare possibility, be conceded now. I can say no more. If you are not afraid of the voyage for yourself, I am not afraid of it (nay, I am all in favour of it on medical grounds) for my patient. What do you say? Will you write to your father and ask him to try what his interest will do with his friends at the Admiralty?'

Mrs Crayford rose excitedly to her feet.

'Write!' she exclaimed. 'I will do better than write. The journey to London is no great matter – and my housekeeper here is to be trusted to take care of Clara in my absence. I will see my father tonight! He shall make good use of his interest at the Admiralty – you may rely on that. Oh, my dear Doctor, what a prospect it is! My husband! Clara! What a discovery you have made – what a treasure you are! How can I thank you?'

'Compose yourself, my dear madam. Don't make too sure of success. We may consider Miss Burnham's objections as disposed of beforehand. But suppose the Lords of the Admiralty say no?'

'In that case, I shall be in London, Doctor; and I shall go to them myself. Lords are only men; and men are not in the habit of saying no to me.'

So they parted.

In a week from that day, Her Majesty's ship *Amazon* sailed for North America. Certain privileged persons, specially interested in the Arctic voyagers, were permitted to occupy the empty staterooms on board. On the list of these favoured guests of the ship were the names of two ladies – Mrs Crayford and Miss Burnham.

CHAPTER SIXTEEN

Once more the open sea – the sea whose waters break on the shores of Newfoundland! An English steamship lies at anchor in the offing. The vessel is plainly visible through the open doorway of a large boathouse on the shore – one of the buildings attached to a fishing station on the coast of the island.

The only person in the boathouse at this moment is a man in the dress of a sailor. He is seated on a chest, with a piece of cord in his hand, looking out idly at the sea. On the rough carpenter's table near him lies a strange object to be left in such a place – a woman's veil.

What is the vessel lying at anchor in the offing?

The vessel is the *Amazon* – dispatched from England to receive the surviving officers and men of the Arctic expedition. The meeting has been successfully effected, on the shores of North America, three days since. But the homeward voyage has been delayed by a storm which has driven the ship out of her course. Taking advantage, on the third day, of the first returning calm, the commander of the *Amazon* has anchored off the coast of Newfoundland, and has sent ashore to increase his supplies of water before he sails for England. The weary passengers have landed for a few hours, to refresh themselves after the discomforts of the tempest. Among them are the two ladies. The veil left on the table in the boathouse is Clara's veil.

And who is the man sitting on the chest, with the cord in his hand, looking out idly at the sea? The man is the only cheerful person in the ship's company. In other words – John Want.

Still reposing on the chest, our friend, who never grumbles, is surprised by the sudden appearance of a sailor at the boathouse door.

'Look sharp with your work there, John Want!' says the sailor. 'Lieutenant Crayford is just coming in to look after you.'

With this warning the messenger disappears again. John Want rises with a groan, turns the chest up on one end, and begins to fasten the cord round it. The ship's cook is not a man to look back on his rescue with the feeling of unmitigated satisfaction which animates his companions in trouble. On the contrary, he is ungratefully disposed to regret the North Pole.

'If I had only known' – thus runs the train of thought in the mind of John Want – 'if I had only known, before I was rescued, that I was to be brought to this place, I believe I should have preferred staying at the North Pole. I was very happy keeping up everybody's spirits at the North Pole. Taking one thing with another, I think I must have been very comfortable at the North Pole – if I had only known it. Another man in my place might be inclined to say that this Newfoundland boathouse was rather a sloppy, slimy, draughty, fishy sort of a habitation to take shelter in. Another man might object to perpetual Newfoundland fogs, perpetual Newfoundland codfish, and perpetual Newfoundland dogs. We had some very nice bears at the North Pole. Never mind! it's all one to me – *I* don't grumble.'

'Have you done cording that box?'

This time the voice is a voice of authority – the man at the doorway is Lieutenant Crayford himself. John Want answers his officer in his own cheerful way.

'I've done it as well as I can, sir – but the damp of this place is beginning to tell upon our very ropes. I say nothing about our lungs – I only say our ropes.'

Crayford answers sharply. He seems to have lost his former relish for the humour of John Want.

'Pooh! To look at your wry face, one would think that our

rescue from the Arctic regions was a downright misfortune. You deserve to be sent back again.'

'I could be just as cheerful as ever, sir, if I *was* sent back again; I hope I'm thankful, but I don't like to hear the North Pole run down in such a fishy place as this. It was very clean and snowy at the North Pole – and it's very damp and sandy here. Do you never miss your bone soup, sir? *I* do. It mightn't have been strong, but it was very hot; and the cold seemed to give it a kind of a meaty flavour as it went down. Was it you that was a-coughing so long last night, sir? I don't presume to say anything against the air of these latitudes; but I should be glad to know it wasn't you that was a-coughing so hollow. Would you be so obliging as just to feel the state of these ropes with the ends of your fingers, sir? You can dry them afterwards on the back of my jacket.'

'You ought to have a stick laid on the back of your jacket. Take that box down to the boat directly. You croaking vagabond! You would have grumbled in the Garden of Eden.'

The philosopher of the expedition was not a man to be silenced by referring him to the Garden of Eden. Paradise itself was not perfect to John Want.

'I hope I could be cheerful anywhere, sir,' said the ship's cook. 'But you mark my words – there must have been a deal of troublesome work with the flower-beds in the Garden of Eden.'

Having entered that unanswerable protest, John Want shouldered the box, and drifted drearily out of the boathouse.

Left by himself, Crayford looked at his watch, and called to a sailor outside.

'Where are the ladies?' he asked.

'Mrs Crayford is coming this way, sir. She was just behind you when you came in.'

'Is Miss Burnham with her?'

'No, sir; Miss Burnham is down on the beach with the passengers.

I heard the young lady asking after you, sir.'

'Asking after me?' Crayford considered with himself as he repeated the words. He added, in lower and graver tones, 'You had better tell Miss Burnham you have seen me here.'

The man made his salute and went out. Crayford took a turn in the boathouse.

Rescued from death in the Arctic wastes, and reunited to a beautiful wife, the lieutenant looked, nevertheless, unaccountably anxious and depressed. What could he be thinking of? He was thinking of Clara.

On the first day when the rescued men were received on board the *Amazon*, Clara had embarrassed and distressed, not Crayford only, but the other officers of the expedition as well, by the manner in which she questioned them on the subject of Francis Aldersley and Richard Wardour. She had shown no signs of dismay or despair when she heard that no news had been received of the two missing men. She had even smiled sadly to herself when Crayford (out of compassionate regard for her) declared that he and his comrades had not given up the hope of seeing Frank and Wardour yet. It was only when the lieutenant had expressed himself in those terms and when it was hoped that the painful subject had been dismissed – that Clara had startled everyone present by announcing that she had something still to say in relation to Frank and Wardour which had not been said yet. Though she spoke guardedly, her next words revealed suspicions of foul play lurking in her mind – exactly reflecting similar suspicions lurking in Crayford's mind – which so distressed the lieutenant, and so surprised his comrades, as to render them quite incapable of answering her. The warnings of the storm which shortly afterwards broke over the vessel were then visible in sea and sky. Crayford made them his excuse for abruptly leaving the cabin in which the conversation had taken place. His brother officers, profiting by his example, pleaded their duties on deck, and followed him out.

On the next day, and the next, the tempest still raged – and the passengers were not able to leave their staterooms. But now, when the weather had moderated and the ship had anchored – now, when officers and passengers alike were on shore, with leisure time at their disposal – Clara had opportunities of returning to the subject of the lost men, and of asking questions in relation to them which would make it impossible for Crayford to plead an excuse for not answering her. How was he to meet those questions? How could he still keep her in ignorance of the truth?

These were the reflections which now troubled Crayford, and which presented him, after his rescue, in the strangely inappropriate character of a depressed and anxious man. His brother officers, as he well knew, looked to him to take the chief responsibility. If he declined to accept it, he would instantly confirm the horrible suspicion in Clara's mind. The emergency must be met, but how to meet it – at once honourably and mercifully – was more than Crayford could tell. He was still lost in his own gloomy thoughts when his wife entered the boathouse. Turning to look at her, he saw his own perturbations and anxieties plainly reflected in Mrs Crayford's face.

'Have you seen anything of Clara?' he asked. 'Is she still on the beach?'

'She is following me to this place,' Mrs Crayford replied.

'I have been speaking to her this morning. She is just as resolute as ever to insist on your telling her of the circumstances under which Frank is missing. As things are, you have no alternative but to answer her.'

'Help me to answer her, Lucy. Tell me, before she comes in, how this dreadful suspicion first took possession of her. All she could possibly have known when we left England was that the two men were appointed to separate ships. What could have led her to suspect that they had come together?'

'She was firmly persuaded, William, that they *would* come together when the expedition left England. And she had read in books of Arctic travel, of men left behind by their comrades on the march, and of men adrift on icebergs. With her mind full of these images and forebodings, she saw Frank and Wardour (or dreamt of them) in one of her attacks of trance. I was by her side; I heard what she said at the time. She warned Frank that Wardour had discovered the truth. She called out to him, "While you can stand, keep with the other men, Frank!" '

'Good God!' cried Crayford; 'I warned him myself, almost in those very words, the last time I saw him!'

'Don't acknowledge it, William! Keep her in ignorance of what you have just told me. She will not take it for what it is – a startling coincidence and nothing more. She will accept it as positive confirmation of the faith, the miserable superstitious faith, that is in her. So long as you don't actually know that Frank is dead, and that he has died by Wardour's hand, deny what she says – mislead her for her own sake – dispute all her conclusions as I dispute them. Help me to raise her to the better and nobler belief in the mercy of God!' She stopped, and looked round nervously at the doorway. 'Hush!' she whispered. 'Do as I have told you. Clara is here.'

CHAPTER SEVENTEEN

Clara stopped at the doorway, looking backwards and forwards distrustfully between the husband and wife. Entering the boathouse, and approaching Crayford, she took his arm, and led him away a few steps from the place in which Mrs Crayford was standing.

'There is no storm now, and there are no duties to be done on board the ship,' she said, with the faint, sad smile which it wrung Crayford's heart to see. 'You are Lucy's husband, and you have an interest in me for Lucy's sake. Don't shrink on that account from giving me pain: I can bear pain. Friend and brother! Will you believe that I have courage enough to hear the worst? Will you promise not to deceive me about Frank?'

The gentle resignation in her voice, the sad pleading in her look, shook Crayford's self-possession at the outset. He answered her in the worst possible manner; he answered evasively.

'My dear Clara,' he said, 'what have I done that you should suspect me of deceiving you?'

She looked him searchingly in the face, then glanced with renewed distrust at Mrs Crayford. There was a moment of silence. Before any of the three could speak again, they were interrupted by the appearance of one of Crayford's brother officers, followed by two sailors carrying a hamper between them. Crayford instantly dropped Clara's arm, and seized the welcome opportunity of speaking of other things.

'Any instructions from the ship, Steventon?' he asked, approaching the officer.

'Verbal instructions only,' Steventon replied. 'The ship will sail with the floodtide. We shall fire a gun to collect the people, and send another boat ashore. In the meantime here are some refreshments for the passengers. The ship is in a state of confusion; the ladies will eat their luncheon more comfortably here.'

Hearing this, Mrs Crayford took *her* opportunity of silencing Clara next.

'Come, my dear,' she said. 'Let us lay the cloth before the gentlemen come in.'

Clara was too seriously bent on attaining the object which she had in view to be silenced in that way. 'I will help you directly,' she answered – then crossed the room and addressed herself to the officer, whose name was Steventon.

'Can you spare me a few minutes?' she asked. 'I have something to say to you.'

'I am entirely at your service, Miss Burnham.'

Answering in those words, Steventon dismissed the two sailors. Mrs Crayford looked anxiously at her husband. Crayford whispered to her, 'Don't be alarmed about Steventon. I have cautioned him; his discretion is to be depended on.'

Clara beckoned to Crayford to return to her.

'I will not keep you long,' she said. 'I will promise not to distress Mr Steventon. Young as I am, you shall both find that I am capable of self-control. I won't ask you to go back to the story of your past sufferings; I only want to be sure that I am right about one thing – I mean about what happened at the time when the exploring party was dispatched in search of help. As I understand it, you cast lots among yourselves who was to go with the party, and who was to remain behind. Frank cast the lot to go.' She paused, shuddering. 'And Richard Wardour,' she went on, 'cast the lot to remain behind. On your honour, as officers and gentlemen, is this the truth?'

'On my honour,' Crayford answered, 'it is the truth.'

'On my honour,' Steventon repeated, 'it is the truth.'

She looked at them, carefully considering her next words, before she spoke again.

'You both drew the lot to stay in the huts,' she said, addressing Crayford and Steventon. 'And you are both here. Richard Wardour drew the lot to stay, and Richard Wardour is not here. How does his name come to be with Frank's on the list of the missing?'

The question was a dangerous one to answer. Steventon left it to Crayford to reply. Once again he answered evasively.

'It doesn't follow, my dear,' he said, 'that the two men were missing together because their names happen to come together on the list.'

Clara instantly drew the inevitable conclusion from that ill-considered reply.

'Frank is missing from the party of relief,' she said. 'Am I to understand that Wardour is missing from the huts?'

Both Crayford and Steventon hesitated. Mrs Crayford cast one indignant look at them, and told the necessary lie, without a moment's hesitation!

'Yes!' she said. 'Wardour is missing from the huts.'

Quickly as she had spoken, she had still spoken too late. Clara had noticed the momentary hesitation on the part of the two officers. She turned to Steventon.

'I trust to your honour,' she said, quietly. 'Am I right, or wrong, in believing that Mrs Crayford is mistaken?'

She had addressed herself to the right man of the two. Steventon had no wife present to exercise authority over him. Steventon, put on his honour, and fairly forced to say something, owned the truth. Wardour had replaced an officer whom accident had disabled from accompanying the party of relief, and Wardour and Frank were missing together.

Clara looked at Mrs Crayford.

'You hear?' she said. 'It is you who are mistaken, not I. What you call "accident", what I call "fate", brought Richard Wardour and Frank together as members of the same expedition, after all.' Without waiting for a reply, she again turned to Steventon, and surprised him by changing the painful subject of the conversation of her own accord.

'Have you been in the Highlands of Scotland?' she asked.

'I have never been in the Highlands,' the lieutenant replied.

'Have you ever read, in books about the Highlands, of such a thing as the Second Sight?'

'Yes.'

'Do you believe in the Second Sight?'

Steventon politely declined to commit himself to a direct reply.

'I don't know what I might have done, if I had ever been in the Highlands,' he said. 'As it is, I have had no opportunities of giving the subject any serious consideration.'

'I won't put your credulity to the test,' Clara proceeded. 'I won't ask you to believe anything more extraordinary than that I had a strange dream in England not very long since. My dream showed me what you have just acknowledged – and more than that. How did the two missing men come to be parted from their companions? Were they lost by pure accident, or were they deliberately left behind on the march?'

Crayford made a last vain effort to check her enquiries at the point which they had now reached.

'Neither Steventon nor I were members of the party of relief,' he said. 'How are we to answer you?'

'Your brother officers who *were* members of the party must have told you what happened,' Clara rejoined. 'I only ask you and Mr Steventon to tell me what they told you.'

Mrs Crayford interposed again, with a practical suggestion this time.

'The luncheon is not unpacked yet,' she said. 'Come, Clara! this is our business, and the time is passing.'

'The luncheon can wait a few minutes longer,' Clara answered. 'Bear with my obstinacy,' she went on, laying her hand caressingly on Crayford's shoulder. 'Tell me how those two came to be separated from the rest. You have always been the kindest of friends – don't begin to be cruel to me now!'

The tone in which she made her entreaty to Crayford went straight to the sailor's heart. He gave up the hopeless struggle: he let her see a glimpse of the truth.

'On the third day out,' he said, 'Frank's strength failed him. He fell behind the rest from fatigue.'

'Surely they waited for him?'

'It was a serious risk to wait for him, my child. Their lives (and the lives of the men they had left in the huts) depended, in that dreadful climate, on their pushing on. But Frank was a favourite. They waited half a day to give Frank the chance of recovering his strength.'

There he stopped. There the imprudence into which his fondness for Clara had led him showed itself plainly, and closed his lips.

It was too late to take refuge in silence. Clara was determined on hearing more.

She questioned Steventon next.

'Did Frank go on again after the half-day's rest?' she asked.

'He tried to go on –'

'And failed?'

'Yes.'

'What did the men do when he failed? Did they turn cowards? Did they desert Frank?'

She had purposely used language which might irritate Steventon into answering her plainly. He was a young man – he fell into the snare that she had set for him.

'Not one among them was a coward, Miss Burnham!' he replied, warmly. 'You are speaking cruelly and unjustly of as brave a set of fellows as ever lived! The strongest man among them set the example; he volunteered to stay by Frank and to bring him on in the track of the exploring party.'

There Steventon stopped – conscious, on his side, that he had said too much. Would she ask him who this volunteer was? No. She went straight on to the most embarrassing question that she had put yet – referring to the volunteer, as if Steventon had already mentioned his name.

'What made Richard Wardour so ready to risk his life for Frank's sake?' she said to Crayford. 'Did he do it out of friendship for Frank? Surely you can tell me that? Carry your memory back to the days when you were all living in the huts. Were Frank and Wardour friends at that time? Did you never hear any angry words pass between them?'

There Mrs Crayford saw her opportunity of giving her husband a timely hint.

'My dear child!' she said; 'how can you expect him to remember that? There must have been plenty of quarrels among the men, all shut up together, and all weary of each other's company, no doubt.'

'Plenty of quarrels!' Crayford repeated; 'and every one of them made up again.'

'And every one of them made up again,' Mrs Crayford reiterated, in her turn. 'There! a plainer answer than that you can't wish to have. Now are you satisfied? Mr Steventon, come and lend a hand (as you say at sea) with the hamper – Clara won't help me. William, don't stand there doing nothing. This hamper holds a great deal; we must have a division of labour. Your division shall be laying the tablecloth. Don't handle it in that clumsy way! You unfold a tablecloth as if you were unfurling a sail. Put the knives on the right, and the forks on the left, and the napkin and the bread between them. Clara, if you are not hungry in this fine air, you ought to be. Come and do your duty; come and have some lunch!'

She looked up as she spoke. Clara appeared to have yielded at last to the conspiracy to keep her in the dark. She had returned slowly to the boathouse doorway, and she was standing alone on the threshold, looking out. Approaching her to lead her to the luncheon table, Mrs Crayford could hear that she was speaking softly to herself. She was repeating the farewell words which Richard Wardour had spoken to her at the ball.

' "A time may come when I shall forgive *you*. But the man who has robbed me of you shall rue the day when you and he first met." Oh, Frank! Frank! does Richard still live, with your blood on his conscience, and my image in his heart?'

Her lips suddenly closed. She started, and drew back from the doorway, trembling violently. Mrs Crayford looked out at the quiet seaward view.

'Anything there that frightens you, my dear?' she asked. 'I can see nothing, except the boats drawn up on the beach.'

'*I* can see nothing either, Lucy.'

'And yet you are trembling as if there was something dreadful in the view from this door.'

'There *is* something dreadful! I feel it, though I see nothing. I feel it, nearer and nearer in the empty air, darker and darker in the sunny light. I don't know what it is. Take me away! No. Not out on the beach. I can't pass the door. Somewhere else! somewhere else!'

Mrs Crayford looked round her, and noticed a second door

at the inner end of the boathouse. She spoke to her husband.

'See where that door leads to, William.'

Crayford opened the door. It led into a desolate enclosure, half garden, half yard. Some nets stretched on poles were hanging up to dry. No other objects were visible – not a living creature appeared in the place. 'It doesn't look very inviting, my dear,' said Mrs Crayford. 'I am at your service, however. What do you say?'

She offered her arm to Clara as she spoke. Clara refused it. She took Crayford's arm, and clung to him.

'I'm frightened, dreadfully frightened!' she said to him, faintly. 'You keep with me – a woman is no protection; I want to be with you.' She looked round again at the boathouse doorway. 'Oh!' she whispered, 'I'm cold all over – I'm frozen with fear of this place. Come into the yard! Come into the yard!'

'Leave her to me,' said Crayford to his wife. 'I will call you if she doesn't get better in the open air.'

He took her out at once, and closed the yard door behind them.

'Mr Steventon, do you understand this?' asked Mrs Crayford. 'What can she possibly be frightened of?'

She put the question, still looking mechanically at the door by which her husband and Clara had gone out. Receiving no reply, she glanced round at Steventon. He was standing on the opposite side of the luncheon table, with his eyes fixed attentively on the view from the main doorway of the boathouse. Mrs Crayford looked where Steventon was looking. This time there was something visible. She saw the shadow of a human figure projected on the stretch of smooth yellow sand in front of the boathouse.

In a moment more the figure appeared. A man came slowly into view, and stopped on the threshold of the door.

CHAPTER EIGHTEEN

The man was a sinister and terrible object to look at. His eyes glared like the eyes of a wild animal; his head was bare; his long grey hair was torn and tangled; his miserable garments hung about him in rags. He stood in the doorway, a speechless figure of misery and want, staring at the well-spread table like a hungry dog. Steventon spoke to him.

'Who are you?'

He answered, in a hoarse, hollow voice:

'A starving man.'

He advanced a few steps, slowly and painfully, as if he were sinking under fatigue.

'Throw me some bones from the table,' he said. 'Give me my share along with the dogs.'

There was madness as well as hunger in his eyes while he spoke those words. Steventon placed Mrs Crayford behind him so that he might be easily able to protect her in case of need, and beckoned to two sailors who were passing the door of the boathouse at the time.

'Give the man some bread and meat,' he said, 'and wait near him.'

The outcast seized on the bread and meat with lean, long-nailed hands that looked like claws. After his first mouthful of the food, he stopped, considered vacantly with himself, and broke the bread and meat into two portions. One portion he put into an old canvas wallet that hung over his shoulder; the other he devoured voraciously. Steventon questioned him.

'Where do you come from?'

'From the sea.'

'Wrecked?'

'Yes.'

Steventon turned to Mrs Crayford.

'There may be some truth in the poor wretch's story,' he said. 'I heard something of a strange boat having been cast on the beach thirty or forty miles higher up the coast. When were you wrecked, my man?'

The starving creature looked up from his food, and made an effort to collect his thoughts – to exert his memory. It was not to be done. He gave up the attempt in despair. His language, when he spoke, was as wild as his looks.

'I can't tell you,' he said. 'I can't get the wash of the sea out of my ears. I can't get the shining stars all night, and the burning sun all day, out of my brain. When was I wrecked? When was I first adrift in the boat? When did I get the tiller in my hand and fight against hunger and sleep? When did the gnawing in my breast, and the burning in my head, first begin? I have lost all reckoning of it. I can't think; I can't sleep; I can't get the wash of the sea out of my ears. What are you baiting me with questions for? Let me eat!'

Even the sailors pitied him. The sailors asked leave of their officer to add a little drink to his meal.

'We've got a drop of grog with us, sir, in a bottle. May we give it to him?'

'Certainly!'

He took the bottle fiercely, as he had taken the food, drank a little, stopped, and considered with himself again. He held up the bottle to the light, and, marking how much liquor it contained, carefully drank half of it only. This done, he put the bottle in his wallet along with the food.

'Are you saving it up for another time?' said Steventon.

'I'm saving it up,' the man answered. 'Never mind what for. That's my secret.'

He looked round the boathouse as he made that reply,

and noticed Mrs Crayford for the first time.

'A woman among you!' he said. 'Is she English? Is she young? Let me look closer at her.'

He advanced a few steps towards the table.

'Don't be afraid, Mrs Crayford,' said Steventon.

'I am not afraid,' Mrs Crayford replied. 'He frightened me at first – he interests me now. Let him speak to me if he wishes it!'

He never spoke. He stood, in dead silence, looking long and anxiously at the beautiful Englishwoman.

'Well?' said Steventon.

He shook his head sadly, and drew back again with a heavy sigh.

'No!' he said to himself, 'that's not *her* face. No! not found yet.'

Mrs Crayford's interest was strongly excited. She ventured to speak to him.

'Who is it you want to find?' she asked. 'Your wife?'

He shook his head again.

'Who, then? What is she like?'

He answered that question in words. His hoarse, hollow voice softened, little by little, into sorrowful and gentle tones.

'Young,' he said; 'with a fair, sad face – with kind, tender eyes – with a soft, clear voice. Young and loving and merciful. I keep her face in my mind, though I can keep nothing else. I must wander, wander, wander – restless, sleepless, homeless – till I find *her!* Over the ice and over the snow; tossing on the sea, tramping over the land; awake all night, awake all day; wander, wander, wander, till I find *her*!'

He waved his hand with a gesture of farewell, and turned wearily to go out.

At the same moment Crayford opened the yard door.

'I think you had better come to Clara,' he began, and

checked himself, noticing the stranger. 'Who is that?'

The shipwrecked man, hearing another voice in the room, looked round slowly over his shoulder. Struck by his appearance, Crayford advanced a little nearer to him. Mrs Crayford spoke to her husband as he passed her.

'It's only a poor, mad creature, William,' she whispered – 'shipwrecked and starving.'

'Mad?' Crayford repeated, approaching nearer and nearer to the man. 'Am *I* in my right senses?' He suddenly sprang on the outcast, and seized him by the throat. 'Richard Wardour!' he cried, in a voice of fury. 'Alive! – alive, to answer for Frank!'

The man struggled. Crayford held him.

'Where is Frank?' he said. 'You villain, where is Frank?'

The man resisted no longer. He repeated vacantly:

'Villain? and where is Frank?'

As the name escaped his lips, Clara appeared at the open yard door, and hurried into the room.

'I heard Richard's name!' she said. 'I heard Frank's name! What does it mean?'

At the sound of her voice the outcast renewed the struggle to free himself with a sudden frenzy of strength which Crayford was not able to resist. He broke away before the sailors could come to their officer's assistance. Halfway down the length of the room he and Clara met one another face to face. A new light sparkled in the poor wretch's eyes; a cry of recognition burst from his lips. He flung one hand up wildly in the air. 'Found!' he shouted, and rushed out to the beach before any of the men present could stop him.

Mrs Crayford put her arms round Clara and held her up. She had not made a movement: she had not spoken a word. The sight of Wardour's face had petrified her.

The minutes passed, and there rose a sudden burst of

cheering from the sailors on the beach, near the spot where the fishermen's boats were drawn up. Every man left his work. Every man waved his cap in the air. The passengers, near at hand, caught the infection of enthusiasm, and joined the crew. A moment more, and Richard Wardour appeared again in the doorway, carrying a man in his arms. He staggered, breathless with the effort that he was making, to the place where Clara stood, held up in Mrs Crayford's arms.

'Saved, Clara!' he cried. 'Saved for *you*!'

He released the man, and placed him in Clara's arms.

Frank! foot-sore and weary – but living – saved; saved for *her*!

'Now, Clara!' cried Mrs Crayford, 'which of us is right? I who believed in the mercy of God? or you who believed in a dream?'

She never answered; she clung to Frank in speechless ecstasy. She never even looked at the man who had preserved him, in the first absorbing joy of seeing Frank alive. Step by step, slower and slower, Richard Wardour drew back, and left them by themselves.

'I may rest now,' he said, faintly. 'I may sleep at last. The task is done. The struggle is over.'

His last reserves of strength had been given to Frank. He stopped – he staggered – his hands waved feebly in search of support. But for one faithful friend he would have fallen. Crayford caught him. Crayford laid his old comrade gently on some sails strewn in a corner, and pillowed Wardour's weary head on his own bosom. The tears streamed over his face. 'Richard! dear Richard!' he said. 'Remember – and forgive me.'

Richard neither heeded nor heard him. His dim eyes still looked across the room at Clara and Frank.

'I have made *her* happy!' he murmured. 'I may lay down my weary head now on the mother earth that hushes all her children to rest at last. Sink, heart! sink, sink to rest! Oh, look at them!' he said to Crayford, with a burst of grief. 'They have forgotten *me* already.'

It was true! The interest was all with the two lovers. Frank was young and handsome and popular. Officers, passengers, and sailors, they all crowded round Frank. They all forgot the martyred man who had saved him – the man who was dying in Crayford's arms.

Crayford tried once more to attract his attention – to win his recognition while there was yet time. 'Richard, speak to me! Speak to your old friend!'

He look round; he vacantly repeated Crayford's last word.

'Friend?' he said. 'My eyes are dim, friend – my mind is dull. I have lost all memories but the memory of *her*. Dead thoughts – all dead thoughts but that one! And yet you look at me kindly! Why has your face gone down with the wreck of all the rest?'

He paused; his face changed; his thoughts drifted back from present to past; he looked at Crayford vacantly, lost in the terrible remembrances that were rising in him, as the shadows rise with the coming night.

'Hark ye, friend,' he whispered. 'Never let Frank know it. There was a time when the fiend within me hungered for his life. I had my hands on the boat. I heard the voice of the Tempter speaking to me: "Launch it, and leave him to die!" I waited with my hands on the boat, and my eyes on the place where he slept. "Leave him! leave him!" the voice whispered. "Love him!" the lad's voice answered, moaning and murmuring in his sleep. "Love him, Clara, for helping *me*!" I heard the morning wind come up in the silence over the great deep. Far and near, I heard the groaning of the floating ice; floating, floating to the clear water and the balmy air. And the wicked Voice floated away with it – away, away, away for ever! "Love him! Love him, Clara, for helping *me*!" No wind could float that away! "Love him, Clara –" '

His voice sank into silence; his head dropped on Crayford's breast. Frank saw it. Frank struggled up on his bleeding feet and parted the friendly throng round him. Frank had not forgotten the man who had saved him.

'Let me go to him!' he cried. 'I must and will go to him! Clara, come with me.'

Clara and Steventon supported him between them. He fell on his knees at Wardour's side; he put his hand on Wardour's bosom.

'Richard!'

The weary eyes opened again. The sinking voice was heard feebly once more.

'Ah! poor Frank. I didn't forget you, Frank, when I came here to beg. I remembered you lying down outside in the shadow of the boats. I saved you your share of the food and drink. Too weak to get at it now! A little rest, Frank! I shall soon be strong enough to carry you down to the ship.'

The end was near. They all saw it now. The men reverently uncovered their heads in the presence of Death. In an agony of despair, Frank appealed to the friends round him.

'Get something to strengthen him, for God's sake! Oh, men! men! I should never have been here but for him! He has given all his strength to my weakness; and now, see how strong I am, and how weak *he* is! Clara, I held by his arm all over the ice and snow. *He* kept watch when I was senseless in the open boat. *His* hand dragged me out of the waves when we were wrecked. Speak to him, Clara! speak to him!' His voice failed him, and his head dropped on Wardour's breast.

She spoke, as well as her tears would let her.

'Richard, have you forgotten me?'

He rallied at the sound of that beloved voice. He looked up at her as she knelt at his head.

'Forgotten you?' Still looking at her, he lifted his hand with an effort, and laid it on Frank. 'Should I have been strong enough to save him if I could have forgotten you?' He waited a moment and turned his face feebly towards Crayford. 'Stay!' he said. 'Someone was here and spoke to me.' A faint light of recognition glimmered in his eyes. 'Ah, Crayford! I recollect now. Dear Crayford! come nearer! My mind clears, but my eyes grow dim. You will remember me kindly for Frank's sake? Poor Frank! why does he hide his face? Is he crying? Nearer, Clara – I want to look my last at *you*. My sister, Clara! Kiss me, sister, kiss me before I die!'

She stooped and kissed his forehead. A faint smile trembled on his lips. It passed away; and stillness possessed the face – the stillness of Death.

Crayford's voice was heard in the silence.

'The loss is ours,' he said. 'The gain is his. He has won the greatest of all conquests – the conquest of himself. And he has died in the moment of victory. Not one of us here but may live to envy *his* glorious death.'

The distant report of a gun came from the ship in the offing, and signalled the return to England and to home.

NOTE ON THE TEXT

The Frozen Deep was originally written as a play by Collins in 1856, and based on Franklin's doomed 1845 expedition to discover the North-West Passage of the Arctic. The play was revised and cast by Dickens, and first performed in January 1857 by Dickens' theatrical company, with Collins and Dickens taking the starring roles of Francis Aldersley and Richard Wardour respectively. Inspired by the notion of the self-sacrificing lover, Dickens went on to create the character of Sydney Carton in his novel, *A Tale of Two Cities* (1859).

In 1874 Collins reworked *The Frozen Deep* into a novella for his reading tour of America. The story first appeared serially in *Temple Bar* from August to October 1874, and was then published in book form as *The Frozen Deep and Other Tales* that same year.

BIOGRAPHICAL NOTE

William Wilkie Collins, author of the first detective novels in English, was born in 1824. The son of a respected landscape painter, he was named after his painter godfather, David Wilkie. Educated in London, Collins studied to become a barrister, although it was never his intention to practise, and by 1848 he had turned to writing, a number of short works appearing in Charles Dickens' periodicals, *Household Words* and, later, *All the Year Round*. A first novel, *Iolani*, set in ancient Tahiti and involving sorcery and sacrifice, though perhaps written as early as 1844, was later rejected by publishers (and only rediscovered and published for the first time in 1999). His second novel, *Antonina* (1850), set in fifth-century Rome, was a popular success, before Collins' first venture into crime fiction with *Basil* (1852), a Gothic tale of doppelgängers, bigamy, and hidden family secrets. Developing at once detective fiction and the novel of sensation, Collins' exotic and gripping stories – often involving strong heroines, sinister locales, charlatans, and physical or psychological afflictions – became hugely popular with the reading public. His great novels appeared in the 1860s, when, at the height of his powers, Collins wrote *The Woman in White* (1860), *No Name* (1863), *Armadale* (1866), and *The Moonstone* (1868).

Unafraid to question Victorian social mores, Collins never married but maintained two families. He lived both with Caroline Graves (whom he met in a midnight encounter such as is described in *The Woman in White*), and with Martha Rudd. In later life, Collins became addicted to opium, and the novels he wrote between 1870 and 1889 (the year he died) are considered inferior to his earlier output.

SELECTED TITLES FROM HESPERUS PRESS

Author	*Title*	*Foreword writer*
Jane Austen	*Love and Friendship*	Fay Weldon
Aphra Behn	*The Lover's Watch*	
Charlotte Brontë	*The Green Dwarf*	Libby Purves
Anton Chekhov	*Three Years*	William Fiennes
Wilkie Collins	*Who Killed Zebedee?*	Martin Jarvis
William Congreve	*Incognita*	Peter Ackroyd
Joseph Conrad	*The Return*	Colm Tóibín
Charles Dickens	*The Haunted House*	Peter Ackroyd
Fyodor Dostoevsky	*The Double*	Jeremy Dyson
George Eliot	*Amos Barton*	Matthew Sweet
Henry Fielding	*Jonathan Wild the Great*	Peter Ackroyd
F. Scott Fitzgerald	*The Rich Boy*	John Updike
Gustave Flaubert	*Memoirs of a Madman*	Germaine Greer
E.M. Forster	*Arctic Summer*	Anita Desai
Elizabeth Gaskell	*Lois the Witch*	Jenny Uglow
Thomas Hardy	*Fellow-Townsmen*	Emma Tennant
L.P. Hartley	*Simonetta Perkins*	Margaret Drabble
Nathaniel Hawthorne	*Rappaccini's Daughter*	Simon Schama
D.H. Lawrence	*Daughters of the Vicar*	Anita Desai
Katherine Mansfield	*In a German Pension*	Linda Grant
Prosper Mérimée	*Carmen*	Philip Pullman
Sándor Petőfi	*John the Valiant*	George Szirtes
Alexander Pope	*The Rape of the Lock*	Peter Ackroyd
Robert Louis Stevenson	*Dr Jekyll and Mr Hyde*	Helen Dunmore
Leo Tolstoy	*Hadji Murat*	Colm Tóibín
Mark Twain	*Tom Sawyer, Detective*	
Oscar Wilde	*The Portrait of Mr W.H.*	Peter Ackroyd
Virginia Woolf	*Carlyle's House and Other Sketches*	Doris Lessing